"You call yourself a lawyer, yet you ignore the facts."

Number one, no one is forcing your grandfather to meet my grandmother. You might ask him who made the first contact. Two, I don't know about your grandfather, but my grandmother is perfectly capable of making her own choices. Nobody will coerce her into doing something she doesn't want to do."

Holly's arguments carried the ring of truth, but Steele didn't care. He had the incredible urge to bang his head against the nearest planter at her blind belief in all this—he glanced around—flowery stuff.

He stalked away. Anger jabbed at him like a hot nail to his heart. Romance was one thing and pink flowers part of it. But turning her romantic notions toward his grandfather, aiding and abetting her desperate grandmother—no way. He would not, could not, in a million years stand by and let those women create a romantic trap to catch his poor grandfather.

LINDA FORD and her husband raised a family of fourteen children, ten adopted, providing her plenty of opportunity to experience God's love and faithfulness. One of her goals in writing is to reveal a little of God's wondrous love through the lives of the people in her stories. She lives in Alberta, Canada, on a ranch she shares with her husband, a paraplegic client, boomerang children, and adorable visiting grandchildren.

Books by Linda Ford

Don't miss out on any of our super romances. Write to us at the following address for information on our newest releases and club information.

Heartsong Presents Readers' Service
PO Box 721
Uhrichsville, OH 44683

Or visit www.heartsongpresents.com

Everlasting Love

Linda Ford

Heartsong Presents

It would seem obvious that I dedicate this book to a couple that has exemplified enduring love. That would be my parents who were devoted to each other throughout life and are now enjoying the glories of heaven together.

But I want to give credit to another kind love—"Love is patient, love is kind." Many people have input into my book after it leaves my hands—people who check content, make sure I haven't had a character get into a car and end up in a truck, and correct my faulty grammar and punctuation. I want to give special credit to one such person: Debbie Cole, freelance copy editor with Heartsong Presents. She does a great job of showing me things I need to do to polish my story. Revisions and edits can be discouraging for the author, but Debbie manages to encourage me through the process. Debbie, thank you for everything you contribute and the spirit in which you do it.

A note from the Author:
I love to hear from my readers! You may correspond with me by writing:

Linda Ford
Author Relations
PO Box 721
Uhrichsville, OH 44683

ISBN 978-1-59789-618-4

EVERLASTING LOVE

Scripture taken from the HOLY BIBLE, NEW INTERNATIONAL VERSION®. NIV®. Copyright © 1973, 1978, 1984 by International Bible Society. Used by permission of Zondervan. All rights reserved.

Our mission is to publish and distribute inspirational products offering exceptional value and biblical encouragement to the masses.

PRINTED IN THE U.S.A.

one

He'd said put him down for something.

He'd specifically mentioned ham or ice cream, but he sure didn't remember agreeing to this.

Steele Davis again read the note his secretary handed him. "Pastor Don says thanks for offering to help with the banquet. The planning committee is meeting at five at J'ava Moi, the café across the street."

No, he had definitely *not* offered to help plan the thing. Not that he couldn't do it. But with the café owner? No way. Something about her he found alarming, disturbing even.

He glanced out the window. There she was in the flesh— Holly Hope—serving a couple at one of her outside tables. Dispensing coffee, smiles, and eternal optimism, her wavy dark hair swinging about her shoulders as she danced her way back into the café.

The whole place screamed romantic nonsense. Practically made a man break into a cold sweat. He hadn't been raised to believe in such stuff, nor had his experience as a lawyer taught him to trust it.

He'd gone for an espresso a few months ago when she first opened her café. Uninvited, she'd told him all about her dreams for the place. "I want to give people a chance to nurture their love. That's why I've created a romantic little spot and named it J'ava Moi. It's a play on words. You know, 'would ya' have me?'"

5

Steele had been fascinated with the way her eyes flashed back and forth between amusement and determination as she talked. He'd also been more than a little awestruck at such a blatant, head-in-the-clouds attitude. As a lawyer, a dealer in realities, he'd felt the need to dispute her optimism. "Not everything can be fixed by flowers and candles."

"I think you'd have to agree it's hard to harbor bitterness while making romantic gestures."

He didn't agree the one canceled out the other and tried again to promote reason. "In my experience, romance doesn't last."

"Maybe because it's neglected." She'd challenged him with a steady look from her dark brown eyes.

To this day he couldn't explain why he didn't just walk away. Maybe it was her denial of facts that made him add, "How many couples do you think I see every year who've vowed before God and man to love each other ' 'til death do them part' and who can now no longer stand the sight of each other? Personally, I will never be fool enough to let emotion overrule reason."

She'd considered him a full, tension-fraught moment then smiled.

The expression made him want to bite the edge off his china cup; it was the same sort of look opposing lawyers gave when they felt they'd argued better and smarter than he—all smug and self-assured.

"Sounds like you have some baggage to deal with," she said with calm assurance as if his life were her business. Which it wasn't.

He remembered clearly how he'd sputtered. He, a lawyer, paid to be good with his mouth, had been at a loss for words.

He'd drained his cup, set it quietly on the table, and resorted to retreat.

He hadn't been back.

Didn't intend to ever return.

Did his best to avoid any contact with the overly cheerful Holly Hope at church.

He glanced again at the paper in his hand. Seems the discussion had been about a banquet as a fund-raiser for some charity. Anxious to get on with his plans for the day, he'd paid little attention to the whole thing—except to offer a food contribution. But if Holly planned it, he could count on lots of hearts and flowers. And if the menu board outside her café indicated her preference, there would be nothing but health food.

Someone needed to make sure she didn't go overboard with the romance nonsense. He checked his watch. Almost five. He had a few minutes before he had to be anywhere. He made up his mind. Steele to the rescue of any innocent man who'd be attending the banquet with a starry-eyed woman at his side.

Besides, how long would it take? He'd give a few suggestions, make sure everyone was on board with a practical plan, then step aside and let someone who *liked* doing this sort of thing take over.

He threw some documents into his briefcase and jogged down the stairs into the warm sunshine.

As he crossed the street, Holly glanced up from cleaning a table and looked startled. "I wasn't sure you'd come."

"Wouldn't miss it for the world." His sarcasm came easily. It'd always been his defense, and something about Holly put him on the defensive.

She straightened and studied him with a glint in her eyes that informed him she doubted he meant what he said. Then she nodded toward a table beside a large potted tree and sheltered by a long planter complete with trellis and drenched in pink flowers.

He shuddered and thought of pulling the table farther along the sidewalk to a place where a man could think.

"Can I bring you something? Espresso, wasn't it?"

How did she remember that? He was so surprised, he sat next to the flowers without protest and for the second time in his life was at a loss for words. All he could manage was a quick nod.

She went inside to get the coffee.

The place oozed romance—a trap to short-circuit a man's reason. He'd just proven it with his little mental lapse.

She returned with two cups and sat across from him. "I expect you'd like to get right to work."

He surely would. Not that he was desperate to get away or anything. He had his thoughts firmly under control. Now. "Shouldn't we wait for the others?"

She laughed.

A pleasant enough sound, but he didn't like the message it conveyed. As if he'd said something supremely foolish.

"We're it."

"The two of us? No way. The pastor said there was a committee."

"Yup. You and me."

He felt her look as much as saw it. Full of challenge. A dare. *Can you handle this, mister?* Of course he could. The sudden beading of sweat across his brow only proved the day was unseasonably warm.

She smiled and wriggled like some kind of overeager pup. "I'm so glad we decided to raise money for the AIDS orphans in Africa. The poor little things. Doesn't it make you want to adopt them all and give them a good home?"

"I doubt the kids would thank you for taking them from their own culture and their familiar world."

Her eager smile flattened. "I *know* that. But it doesn't stop me from wishing I could do more." She looked down and toyed with her cup.

His chest felt stiff at the way her enthusiasm had died. What was the matter with him? He wasn't usually so argumentative outside the courtroom.

He drew in a deep breath full of a jumble of scents— honey, cinnamon, and other spices he couldn't name. He couldn't tell if the smells came from the flowers, the cookies and muffins in the display case, or a combination of both.

He was thankful she spoke again, pulling him from considering the source of the intriguing aromas and back to the subject at hand.

"To start with, we need a theme. I thought something like 'For the love of—'"

He rolled his eyes.

She stopped. "You don't like that?" Again that long, considering look. "Am I sensing a problem here?"

"It isn't a Valentine banquet. If we must have a theme, let's make it something more appropriate like"—he did some quick mental gymnastics—"'Aid for AIDS victims.'" He smiled, pleased he'd managed to come up with something in such a hurry. "It's simple and practical."

She tipped her head, a brittle gleam in her eyes. "It sounds like a newspaper headline. We need something a little catchier."

"What's wrong with newspaper headlines? They say things succinctly. No guessing as to what it's all about."

"Let's keep thinking about it. Maybe we'll come up with something better."

He knew what she really meant. Not something better—something *she* liked. He could see this was going to be about as much fun as stepping on a nail.

She nodded briskly. "Let's move on then. What about decorations?"

He gave a long, deliberate look around the place. "We could maybe skip the frilly and flowery. How about something—" Again he had to scramble for a substitute.

"You don't like the way I've decorated the café?"

Intuition was supposedly a woman's strength, but right now he had a sudden flash of understanding and knew he'd offended the woman.

"It's very pretty. Just a little too. . ." Pink. He glanced around. Apart from the flower cart, now almost empty, and the bank of pink to his right, there wasn't as much of the color as he pictured. In fact, he saw lots of green, some kind of tan color that probably had a fancy name, and black wrought-iron furniture. "It's a little too"—he was stuck for words again—"romantic," he blurted.

"So you don't believe in love."

"Of course I do, but the biblical sort. Love is patient, kind, gentle, and forgiving—keeps no record of wrongs. As I see it, love is practical. It doesn't need all these trappings to be real."

She snorted. A very expressive sound, communicating quite effectively her disbelief. "So it's romance you object to." She favored him with a smile.

If her smile had been mocking, he would have known

how to react, but it was full of sweet patience and slid right past his sarcasm and defensiveness. Left him speechless. Again. Not that she seemed to notice. She went right on as if intent on exploring the whole realm of psychology as per Steele Davis.

"That's a curious belief. I'm guessing it's more personal than dealing with angry couples seeking a divorce. Any chance you've been married?"

"Not me."

She struck out on that one.

"Your parents then? Are they divorced?"

"Nope." Strike two. "My parents have what I consider a very good marriage. It's not based on dreams. It's—"

"Practical?" She pulled her mouth down into a fierce frown. "A business arrangement maybe?"

"What's wrong with that?"

"Sounds cold and calculating."

"Not to me. It sounds sensible and lasting."

"And safe. But no risks, no glory."

He didn't like the way this conversation had headed south. How had she turned it from banquet plans to dissecting his parents' marriage and examining his motivation for disliking romance? Not caring for a whole lot of sentimentality didn't point to his having a deep, dark secret—just a long streak of practical. "About the decorations. . ."

"Not you. Not your parents."

"Maybe we could have something solid. Like—"

But she would not be sidetracked. He was beginning to think she'd missed her calling. She should have been a lawyer.

"A sibling then?"

Cold filled his insides. Cold, blue anger at her persistence, at being forced to admit, if only to himself, how Mike's divorce had hurt him. Hurt the whole family. He was still helping Mike clean up from it. Becky had practically destroyed them and could have destroyed the family business if Steele hadn't fought her every step of the way. Even so, it had cost them a bundle.

Steele and Mike had both sworn off women, but Bill, only twenty-four and six years younger than Steele, was unable to get past his hurt and anger at how Becky had treated them. He spent his time pursuing women only to dump them before they could dump him. Everyone in the family knew what he was doing, but they couldn't make Bill understand how irresponsible his behavior was.

It filled Steele with frustration to see his brothers trying to come to grips with their anger, though Steele preferred anger to the bouts of depression that so often gripped Mike.

Holly's smile faded. "I'm sorry. I didn't mean to hit a nerve. Let's get back to planning the banquet." She paused as if knowing he needed a minute to pull his thoughts back to the business at hand.

He wanted to resent her prodding more than he appreciated her insight and kindness, but it proved a difficult choice.

She seemed to know when he'd pushed away the intense emotion grabbing his throat. "Now about the decorations. I think we need to keep in mind this is a formal, dressy affair. People will expect something rather special. I thought a summer theme like a garden room. Banks of flowers and greenery. . ." She paused as if reading his mind.

Or maybe she simply saw the way his lips curled as he

interrupted her. "I suppose lots and lots of pink flowers and pink and white balloons. You know a man could get some kind of fever with all that pink."

She narrowed her eyes as if to argue then suddenly chuckled.

The sound surprised him—a deep-throated trill like some kind of cheery songbird.

"But that's just what I had in mind—love fever."

He shuddered. "It's not something to joke about. There's nothing romantic or sensible about a couple with stars in their eyes and their brains out of gear." He'd seen over and over how it led to disaster.

She chuckled again.

And again he felt a sudden internal lurch at the sound. He shook his head to clear it, though the confusion seemed to originate from an unfamiliar place behind his heart. Something he was loath to admit even to himself.

She grew serious. "I say pink flowers, lots of greenery, maybe some streamers. We want to make it special."

"That's your idea of special, not mine." He glanced around the outdoor seating area and shot a pained look through the door to more flowers and fancy stuff.

Her brown eyes turned as cold as the soil on his grandfather's ranch in the dead of winter. "I'll have you know that many people, men and women alike, find my décor very relaxing, very romantic."

"Exactly. Could we skip romantic and go straight to something ordinary?"

She made an exasperated sound. "If people wanted ordinary, they would stay in their own backyards and save themselves the cost of a banquet. It has to be special somehow."

"Isn't that where the food comes in?"

"We also need entertainment, decorations, other things."

"Entertainment? Whoa." He glanced at his watch and saw his plans for a quick appearance disappear in a flash. "I thought the career group simply wanted to do something special for the summer."

"It's more than just something to do."

Remembering her impassioned argument at the meeting, wanting to turn the event into a fund-raiser, he guessed he couldn't blame her for sounding defensive any more than he could stop the sudden clenching of his gut at the idea of spending hours with this woman, arguing about minutia. He couldn't imagine how they'd work together. Her belief in romance grated against the facts he witnessed day after day. But with admirable determination, considering his long sigh of exasperation, she pushed on.

"I wanted to do something to benefit the AIDS victims. Something wonderful to get everyone involved."

"R—i—g—h–t." He waved around the empty café. "Let's get everyone involved. Oh, wait. You and I are everyone, and I didn't even offer to help plan the thing. I thought I could contribute something in the way of food or help set up." What had Pastor Don been thinking to assign him to help on a committee of two? He mentally shrugged. Likely the same as he—someone had to make sure this banquet didn't turn into a lovefest.

"So you're not behind this?"

"No." He backtracked as her hard look silently accused him of withholding food from a starving child. "I mean, yes, of course I'm behind it. I just hadn't planned to be in charge. Not that I mind helping. In fact I probably have a lot to contribute." *Yeah. Uh huh. Like what?* He hoped she didn't have the same thought.

"Really?" No mistaking the disbelief in her voice. "Then perhaps you'd like to be in charge of entertainment."

Then again maybe not. "I figure if you intend to hire a professional group of any sort, you should have done it months ago."

"No, if *you* want to hire a group. . .didn't we just agree you'd look after entertainment?"

"Holly, I did not agree to anything except bringing ice cream. But I'm here, and I can see you need help."

She snorted.

"I admit," he said, "I haven't given the whole thing a lot of thought." *None, in fact.* "But I'm prepared to do my part. Why don't I look after decorations and *you* arrange entertainment?"

She laughed out loud—the sound a mixture of horror and amusement that managed to scratch his nerve endings at the same time as it tickled the unfamiliar spot deep inside.

"I don't think so. I want this banquet to be memorable."

They stared at each other, his gaze, he suspected, as hard and unyielding as hers. He wanted nothing more than to hand the whole business over to her and let her do what she wanted. But his stubborn, practical side warned him he wouldn't be happy with himself or the results if he did. He owed it to the pastor, to the church members, and to the male populace as a whole to keep Holly from inflicting her sentimental notions on them.

"Very well," he conceded reluctantly. "We'll work together."

Boy, did she look happy about that. Yeah, right. She pulled her pretty pink lips down in the most daunting frown.

"That's an oxymoron if I ever heard one. You and I 'work

together.' Why don't we just go to Pastor Don and ask him to replace you?"

"Why? It's not as if I don't have the brains to help plan a simple little banquet. We'll work together just fine." No way would he let anyone tell him he couldn't do it.

"You're sure? You won't just sneer at every one of my ideas and do your best to ruin the whole affair?"

He'd never been more certain he did *not* want to do something. Except maybe for the time he'd been forced to take dancing classes at school and had to dance with Penny, the prettiest girl in class. He'd broken out in hives every time her hand touched his. Come to think of it, this situation wasn't a lot different. He'd survived the Penny torture. And now he was all grown up—a lawyer who did not flinch at anything. "Why would I want to ruin things? I'll help. This will be the best banquet you've ever seen."

"Then we need to get down to work."

"Right. I'd say the most pressing is entertainment. When did you say the banquet will be?"

She gave a date less than two months away.

"Who can we possibly get at such short notice?"

She lifted her hand in an airy wave. "We don't have to hire entertainers. We could have a talent show."

He groaned. "I can just see it. Mr. Alaston reciting 'The Rime of the Ancient Mariner' and Grandma Moses singing 'Amazing Grace.'" Now that's memorable all right. But probably not the way you'd like it to be."

She laughed. "Her name is Mrs. Pocklington."

Funny, he'd never noticed before what a heartwarming laugh she had. Likely because he'd been so busy avoiding her.

She sobered, but her eyes continued to dance with amusement. "Then what do you suggest? I think it has to be local because of the time constraints; but also, the more people personally contribute, the more they will be invested in the whole purpose of this banquet—helping the orphans."

He glanced at his watch. "Hey, I've got to run." He had a six-thirty appointment. "We'll need to continue this. I'll give it some thought, and we'll meet again."

"When? Or are you already changing your mind about helping?"

He stood and gave her a mocking grin. "Are you always so suspicious?"

She didn't answer, but the look she gave remained challenging. "When?"

"Tomorrow?" At her nod he tried to recall his appointments but couldn't. "I'll check my schedule and let you know what works."

"Of course." She sounded resigned, as if she expected him to be a no-show.

"I'm serious."

"Then I'll see you tomorrow."

He nodded and jogged toward his red SUV.

Halfway home it hit him. He'd just committed to spending time with a confirmed romantic. The same woman he'd spent several months avoiding because of her blatantly obvious sentimentality.

He groaned.

Hey, wait a minute, man. You survived Penny when you were thirteen; you can survive Holly when you're almost thirty.

two

The next day, Holly pushed her planters out to the sidewalk and paused to sniff deeply of the scented purple pansies— sweet as new love. She gave a satisfied glance around. She loved her café. She had decorated it like a garden retreat, hoping to give it a bit of a European flair.

She aimed to provide coffee that made her customers sigh with contentment and sandwiches and snacks to rev up their taste buds, but she wanted to do even more. She wanted to give them hope, show them how to keep love thriving, and maybe show them a glimpse of God's great love.

Perhaps to some it sounded unrealistic, naïve even.

Steele clearly thought along those lines.

She stole a glance toward the windows of his office. The first time he'd sauntered over for coffee shortly after she opened, she'd recognized him from church and asked where he worked. He'd pointed out his office windows. They had the kind of glass you couldn't see through from the outside. Not that she wanted to see him. What did it matter what he thought? Yet she felt a burning desire to prove him wrong about romance. But even more, whatever had happened that brought such sudden pain to his eyes yesterday, he needed to know the hurt could be healed. She realized she had pressed her hands to her chest, and immediately dropped them. His pain was not her pain.

She put the donation jar next to the cash register and

paused to look at the pictures she'd glued to it. A great yawning sense of futility hit her as she touched the faces of the children—orphans in South Africa, their parents victims of the AIDS scourge. All her tips went into this jar as well as whatever people felt like donating. It was so little, but now with the proceeds from the banquet. . . *Lord, help it go well. Help us raise enough to repair the building.*

Her friend Heather worked with the orphans. In almost every e-mail, she mentioned the need to repair the building. It was impossible to keep the children, let alone the supplies, dry during the wet season. Holly had privately promised to raise enough money for the job before the next rainy season. She was counting on this banquet. She had her own plans for it—local involvement, special atmosphere, good food. She wouldn't let Steele's objections ruin it for her and, ultimately, the orphans.

The morning rush began, and she had little time to worry about Steele. She and Annie, her morning assistant, kept busy right through the lunch hour. It finally slowed down midafternoon. She mixed up a fresh batch of muffins, a new recipe full of all sorts of nutritious things—sunflower seeds, grated orange, cranberries, and slivered almonds. As she slipped them into the oven, she heard someone enter and went to wait on her customer.

Steele. She faltered. Somehow, despite his assurance he'd help, she'd doubted he would return. But there he stood, eyeing the muffins and cookies in the display case.

"You have anything here but health food?"

She moved forward, smiling. Although her food wasn't technically health food, she often got that initial reaction. Her customers changed their minds after the first taste. "Just because it's healthy doesn't mean it tastes bad."

He looked unconvinced.

"My favorite is the sunshine muffin. Why don't you try one? I guarantee it won't kill you."

"Right. What you're saying is I'll survive. Now that sounds appealing. What does it have in it?"

She laughed at his look of uncertainty. "I can't tell you the exact ingredients, of course. That's one of my trade secrets. But it is moist and rich in flavor. May I get you one?"

Looking as if he'd agreed to being stabbed with a sword, he nodded. "And an espresso."

She filled the order and handed it to him.

He glanced about the café. There were only three other customers. "Can we talk?"

She hesitated. She'd been looking forward to a break and a chance to enjoy the sunshine and the scent of her flowers, but dealing with Steele's arguments would ruin her enjoyment of nature. She studied her donation jar. For the orphans, she reminded herself. "I can spare a few minutes. Why don't we sit outside?" She followed him with a coffee for herself.

He waited until she sat down before he bit into his muffin. Surprise, enjoyment, disbelief chased each other across his face.

She laughed until her eyes watered.

Finally he sighed. "This is good."

"Just like I said."

"You did."

She chose to ignore the surprise in his voice. "So have you had any more ideas for the banquet?"

He drank some coffee before he continued. "I've been thinking."

"Good. So have I. If you insist on helping, I can't stop you. After all, it's not my private thing. But I won't relent on what I consider the essentials."

"Yeah, I got that already. So here's my plan. We'll do some brainstorming. Each of us contributes until we find a plan we both agree on. It's the only way I can see this is going to work."

She groaned. "It's a great plan, Steele, but the banquet is supposed to be this summer. Not next century."

He slowly put his cup down and grinned. "Is it that bad?"

"I'm sure you've noticed we tend to disagree."

He suddenly leaned forward. "Seeing as it's for a good cause, I guess we'll just have to concentrate on the task at hand and forget our differences."

She met his gaze. She'd noticed his eyes the first day he wandered over full of doubt and curiosity. Unusual eyes, beautiful even, light hazel that subtly changed color, sometimes green, other times, like now, almost brown. She hoped the soft color meant he truly intended to get behind this project. On her part, she'd cooperate as much as possible. "We can try."

He looked surprised, as if expecting her to disagree, and then he laughed. "All right then."

She stared. His amusement was unexpected. Not only that, his laugh tickled up and down her spine, filled her chest with something she couldn't name. She might have called it shock, but it had a distinctly pleasant feel to it.

He glanced at his watch. "I'm out of time for now. When shall we do this brainstorming?"

"Why don't you come back here when you're finished at your office?" She'd even sweeten the offer with a promise of an early dinner. "We can eat and work at the same time."

He glanced at his empty plate where his healthy muffin had once sat. He looked doubtful. "I'm really not into health food."

She stuffed back annoyance at his blatant prejudice. Did he resist everything outside his normal experience? The man must live an extraordinarily boring life if he did. But sick of defending her food, her café, and her belief in love, she flicked her hand in a dismissive gesture. "Order something delivered if it makes you feel any better."

He didn't answer and had the decency to look uncomfortable, but she didn't give him a chance to provide any more excuses or arguments.

"What time should I expect you?" she asked.

He got to his feet. "I don't have any late appointments. Would five be okay?"

"Of course." She answered without giving herself a chance to think about it, because if she did, she'd be saying no. She had the uneasy feeling she'd regret working with him no matter how it turned out. She imagined continual arguments, more of his criticism of her belief in the value of romance, and, worst of all, more of that funny, happy, delicious feeling when he looked at her with surprise in his eyes. No, she could tell this wasn't going to turn out well.

She waited for him to cross the street then hurried in to stare at the little faces on the donation jar. She'd do whatever it took, even work with Steele. But she intended to be prepared.

"Annie, can you manage on your own for a few minutes? I'm going to dash home and pick up something."

&

She was armed and ready when he appeared on the sidewalk.

It was a lovely afternoon, so she'd taken her arsenal out to one of the outdoor tables. But he went past her into the café and stood in front of the display case.

"Did you order something to eat?"

He shot her a look, half grin, half grimace. "Decided to be brave and try something here." He checked out the remaining sandwiches.

The selection was pretty limited. Only two remained—a vegetarian and a wasabi roast beef. She chuckled at the way he tried to hide his distress.

"You wouldn't happen to have just a simple roast beef sandwich?"

"Wasabi is Japanese horseradish that usually accompanies sushi," she explained. "Be brave. Try it. If you don't like it, I'll refund your money."

Obviously not overjoyed at the prospect, he nodded. "Sure. I'll have it."

She pulled out the two remaining sandwiches—she'd eat the vegetarian—and poured them each a coffee. He offered to take the tray, but she shook her head and carried the food to one of the outside tables.

She waited until he bit into his sandwich, waited for him to decide if he liked it, grinned when his eyes widened and he sighed. "Good. Just like you said."

For a few minutes, they discussed the weather and made conversational noises. But as soon as he finished his sandwich, she pushed aside the rest of hers and pulled the papers toward her. "I want to show you something." She handed him the first page.

He stared at the picture of the ten-year-old girl Heather had sent. "What is this?"

"One of the orphans I want to help." She explained about Heather's work. As she talked, she handed him more pictures and repeated the stories Heather had told her. "Some of these children have cared for parents dying of the disease. Then they are alone trying to support themselves. Many of them have never had anyone teach them the skills they need to survive on their own."

"I've heard about the situation." He put the pictures aside. "You are showing me these for what purpose?"

She nodded. Should have known his lawyer brain would see through her ploy. "I hoped if you could put faces to the project, you'd understand why it's so important to me that this banquet succeed in a big way."

He had a way of studying her that seemed calculated to expose any pretense, but she had none. From the first, she'd been bluntly honest about her intention that this banquet must be special.

"You're saying it's more than entertainment for you and you want me to have the same commitment to a noble cause?"

She nodded, uncertain if he liked the idea or found it more of what he'd consider her idealistic, unrealistic romantic nonsense.

His eyes lightened to amber, and he smiled, filling his face with sudden agreement. "I'd say we both want the banquet to succeed. Our problem is in how each of us thinks is the best way to achieve that."

"Thank you. Now I've done some thinking. A banquet needs a number of things. I mentioned them before. Special decorations, good food and entertainment. I want local entertainers because it gets people more personally involved and because we don't have time or money to bring in a group."

"You did mention theme yesterday."

"Right. Theme has a twofold purpose—it informs people of the cause and gives us something we can build everything else around."

"Aid for AIDS. That about covers it, I think."

She resisted the urge to roll her eyes. She'd done a lot of thinking about this and realized as a lawyer he needed facts, not feelings, to convince him. "It isn't quite the idea I want to convey. Makes it sound as if there will be a lot of pressure to give. We need something a little more upbeat."

He drummed his fingers on the table and looked into the distance. "Aid, aid, aid. How about band aid?"

This time she groaned. "Sure, and we'll drape tape and dressings all around for decoration."

He leaned forward. "Not that kind of band-aid. Hear me out while I think this through. Band—bands. Marching bands. Band AID. Band entertainment. By setting specifics for a talent show, we could eliminate Grandma Moses and that type of thing. There's a lot of talent in the church and community. Enough for several bands. Anyone who wants can form one. We'll have a band playoff. Like that TV show, *American Idol*. The crowd votes one band out at a time until we have the new 'Band Idol.'"

She hadn't expected anything but arguments and opposition from him, but surprised as she was to admit it, this was a good idea. "What about decorations?" He'd made it clear he wanted nothing frilly, aka romantic.

"Bunting. Like an old-fashioned political rally. Lots and lots of red, white, and blue bunting."

She'd have never thought of it. "Did you spend the afternoon thinking about this?"

"Nope. Just came up with it. It's called brainstorming. You start throwing out ideas, think about words—"

She'd prayed for unity on this project. She'd prayed for God to bless the planning. This had to be a gift from Him. Even if He chose to send it through a man who openly mocked her on things she held near and dear. She gave a prayer of silent thanks and breathed in a request for strength to be cooperative. She smiled. "I like your ideas. We could keep the food in theme by serving red, white, and blue."

"No health food."

"Why not? We could do tofu with a red tomato sauce and a blueberry salad." She laughed at the shocked look on his face. "Steele, I'm kidding."

He let out a whoof. "Glad to hear that."

An hour later they'd come up with a menu they both agreed on—meat of some sort, baked potatoes, salads, desserts—Holly agreed to contact a caterer. She planned to suggest salads and desserts that would continue the theme. They'd drafted an announcement to go out to the various churches for the band competition. Steele had insisted he'd locate the material for decorations. Holly understood he didn't trust her not to turn it into something lovey-dovey.

Meggie, her afternoon assistant, poked her head out. "Shall I close up?"

Holly checked her watch, surprised at how the time had flown. "It's late. You run along. I'll close."

Steele got to his feet. "I think we have it organized for now, but I suppose we'll need to keep in touch as things develop."

"Right." She waited until he gathered his stuff before she started to pull things into the café.

He paused, dropped his briefcase on a chair, and grabbed the planter to push it inside.

"You don't need to help. It's my job. I can do it."

"I'm just being practical. If you hurt yourself, it leaves me to handle the banquet on my own." He grinned at her. "I'm not saying I couldn't do it, but. . ." He shrugged.

She thanked him, tipping her head down to hide the confusion his grin triggered in her. She was used to him as an adversary, not a friend. Having him act as if it mattered whether or not she needed help, even if only to protect her position as the other committee member, weakened her resistance to him. Now why that should matter, she couldn't say. It wasn't as if they were destined to become soul mates.

She chuckled at the idea, felt his curious look, and grinned at him. "You'd no doubt manage just fine."

three

Steele tilted his chair back and let out a long, weary sigh.

It had been another of those mind-numbing, go-for-the-throat sessions. Despite both his mediation and the other lawyer's, it seemed the husband and wife were determined to do the most damage before they ended their marriage. This couple attended the same church he did, but it no longer shocked him to have believers come in for a divorce. Or maybe it did. But the vindictiveness left him shaking his head. If they felt the need to end their relationship, couldn't they do it calmly, efficiently?

He closed his eyes and rested his head on the back of his soft leather chair.

As a lawyer, he should take up something less draining—like defending serial killers.

Lethargy sucked at his bones. With a great effort, he opened his eyes and looked out the window, hoping to see some activity at the little café. He always got a chuckle out of watching Holly at work.

He'd spent far more time across the street in the past few weeks than in the entire six months she'd been there. They'd had to discuss all sorts of things to do with the banquet. How many guests could they expect? What was the upper limit? How many bands? Entry fees. Prizes. Choosing salads and desserts from the selection the caterer suggested.

Steele bolted to his feet. "I need a coffee," he muttered to himself and headed across the street. He chose an outside table against the window.

Holly hurried out with his usual espresso. Without waiting for an invitation, she pulled out the chair across from him and plunked herself down. "I saw the Bensons leaving your office." She mentioned the couple from church that had been in his office a few minutes ago.

He studied her over the top of his cup. "Have a chair."

Her startled laugh and faint blush made him smile. "Don't mind if I do," she said.

"I'm not the only office in the building."

"Maybe not, but not many people come out of the camera shop with murder in their eyes." She sat back, crossed her arms, and studied him.

He returned her look for look, attitude for attitude. She had her own peculiar ideas of how he should run his business. On several occasions he'd come close to being rude about her suggestions but instead restrained himself to pointing out it was a little late to hand out flowers by the time couples sought out lawyers. He got a kick from the way she always sprang to the defense of her romantic notions. He probably shouldn't enjoy teasing her as much as he did.

"Did you recommend a counselor to them?" she demanded.

He said nothing. After all, Mr. Benson was a client and entitled to his privacy even in downtown Missoula, Montana, where everyone seemed to know everyone else's business. But, no, he hadn't recommended counseling. He gave her a sad frown and shook his head. Maybe she'd give him one of her sunshine-drenched smiles if she thought he regretted the oversight. In his experience, though, people had to want to work things out. And if they didn't, trying to reason with them was futile.

She shifted her gaze away. He felt a momentary relief to be free of her concentrated study, but then she pinned him again, her eyes hard as ice. "It's just wrong."

He cocked one eyebrow. She'd never made any secret of what she thought about this part of his job. "Good coffee."

She served the perfect cup of coffee—hot enough to scald his tongue, strong enough to fuel jet planes.

That and the fact they had the banquet to plan were the only reasons he came here. Their worlds were light-years apart. Or perhaps, more accurately, their philosophies. She, a confirmed romantic; he, a practical lawyer who dealt with realities.

A tourist couple, complete with digital cameras they aimed indiscriminately, parked themselves at a table half-hidden by the potted flowers.

Holly spared him one more "how could you?" look that had as much impact as a slap with invisible paper, then rushed to wait on the couple.

"Welcome. And what brings you to Missoula?"

The couple admitted they were on their honeymoon. Steele sat back to listen to the conversation, smiling widely at Holly's predictable response. He'd seen her in action before.

"Congratulations." She selected three pink flowers from the cart she refilled every morning and handed them a card along with the tiny bouquet.

The young woman gushed over it. "How sweet. Did you paint this yourself?" She indicated the front of the card.

Holly laughed. "It's a hobby of mine. That and collecting sayings to include."

The new wife opened the card and read aloud, " 'How do

I love thee? Let me count the ways. I love thee to the depth and breadth and height my soul can reach.' That's so special. Look, honey." She handed it to her husband.

He took the card, read it, and smiled adoringly at the young woman at his side before he lifted his gaze to Holly. "Do you do this for all your customers?"

"I believe in doing my part to keep love alive and well."

The newlyweds drank in each other's presence, and the woman whispered, "Our love is solid as a rock."

Steele studied their clasped hands, watched as the woman buried her nose in the bouquet, her gaze never leaving her husband, and felt a strange, empty hunger—a yawning ache deep inside.

Holly brought their coffee and left them to return to Steele. "Can I get you something to eat?"

He realized he'd forgotten to have lunch. No wonder he had such an empty feeling inside. "Do you have any of those roast beef sandwiches left?"

"Sure do."

Another reason he kept returning. The first time he'd read the name of the sandwich—wasabi roast beef—he'd grimaced. He'd studied the already-prepared sandwiches in the display case. And then she'd challenged him to try it. Her coffee-brown eyes seemed to dare him, and he wasn't about to turn down a dare, especially from a pretty young woman. From the first bite, he was hooked. The tender beef was sliced thin. The wasabi had enough zest to give the sandwich a delicious bite without clearing his sinuses. The sliced ripe tomato and crisp lettuce provided just the right amount of textural interest and coolness. It was the kind of sandwich that made him smile and lick his fingers when he finished.

Right now his mouth watered in anticipation.

She returned with the sandwich and a generous square of carrot cake spread with cream cheese frosting.

The young couple finished their coffee, called thanks, and wandered away, arm in arm. Steele wondered how much they saw of the sights of Missoula. They seldom took their gazes off each other.

"I love to see newlyweds," Holly said.

He picked up the sandwich and heard the wasabi and roast beef call his name, but he couldn't ignore her blind optimism. He hesitated a moment then said, "I wish them all the best, but the odds are against them, you know."

She sat down at his table again. "Steele, it's a pity you see only the disasters, but surely you've seen long-lasting marriages, full of romance."

He savored the flavor of his sandwich, too distracted by his hunger to think about her question.

"I know you said your parents have a practical relationship, but surely they have little romantic things they do."

He wiped his mouth and drank from the glass of water she'd provided. Finally, unable to avoid her probing gaze, he answered. "My parents aren't the least bit romantic." At her doubtful look, he added, "Unless you count running for parts for each other or changing the oil in one of the Cats." He chuckled at the way her eyes widened in surprise.

"A kitty cat?"

"No, a Caterpillar machine. Think tracks and lots of noise and bounce. As I said, my parents have a businesslike relationship. It works extremely well." He grinned as he watched her digest this information. Loved the way it shook her concept of marriage.

She blinked away the idea and shook her head as if his parents' marriage relationship didn't count. "I wish you could see my parents together. I think it would change your mind about romance."

He felt a flash of annoyance. Some people simply refused to accept any idea that didn't support their chosen belief. As a lawyer, he didn't have that luxury. Not that he'd allow such fuzzy thinking even if he drove a Cat D9 for a living. Time to change the subject.

"How many entries do you have for the band competition?"

"Four so far. How many are we going to accept?"

"Four? I never expected that many."

"O ye of little faith. From the beginning I've prayed for this to be a huge success."

"As if I didn't know that." She never let him forget it. "Hadn't we better limit it? Seems four is about all we can manage. We might have to change the voting thing. It's going to take too long to eliminate them one by one."

"Aww. I wanted to do the TV thing."

He checked for the telltale spark in her eyes, saw it, and knew she teased. "How about a three-round elimination?"

She shrugged. "If we can't vote them out one by one, I don't care how we do it."

He laughed. It hadn't taken him long to discover she had an irrepressible need to tease. One thing in her favor. About the only thing. Except maybe her dedication to a cause. He admired that in anyone.

Whoa, who's tallying points here? They were as opposite as day and night, as compatible as oil and water. The only thing they shared was the desire to make this banquet a success, each for their own reasons. She, because of her personal involvement with an African orphanage. He, because he didn't like to admit defeat in anything.

He headed back to his office a few minutes later, thankful they had the banquet plans well under way. They had no need to spend a lot of time together until last-minute jobs demanded attention.

❧

Holly stepped out of the back door of the café and locked up behind herself. She headed down the alley toward historic East Pine Street, where she lived. She loved Missoula. Full of flowers and trees, it deserved its nickname as the garden city. She'd loved it even before her first glimpse of the straw-colored hills crowned with emerald pines against a backdrop of smoky-blue mountains.

From when Holly was young, her grandmother had filled her vivid imagination with magical tales of a year spent in Missoula as nanny to a family who lived in one of the prestigious East Pine Street houses. Her grandmother told her of romantic walks along the river, picnics on the beautiful university campus. It was Nan's tales that had sent Holly from her home in Kalispell to Missoula, first to Montana U to get her business degree, then to buy the shop where she'd started her café—part of her dream come true. The other part of her dream had been achieved when she got an apartment in the historic Steigl complex.

She paused outside the building where she lived. She loved its genteel atmosphere with the brick exterior and the gentle arches on the first-story windows. She loved the leisurely, friendly feel of the city.

She climbed to her second-story apartment, grabbed her laptop, and headed for the chaise lounge on the balcony overlooking the street. She gave a satisfied sigh. Plans for the banquet were well in hand. Life was good. God was good.

She fired up her computer and started to type an e-mail.

Hey, Heather,

How's it goin', girl? Any more centipedes breaking into your mosquito netting? Please don't send me any more pictures of them. Ugh. I couldn't sleep for two days imagining one of them crawling over me. (Okay, it was only two minutes, but just the same—<shudder>)

I told you how I managed to sneak my colorful choice of salads under Steele's radar. All the man cared about was the portion size of the meat. He almost nixed the chicken in favor of steak, but the caterers don't do steak.

I want to do a slide show featuring you and your work. You don't have any objection, do you? Perhaps you can help me with it. Send me a bunch of pictures. Or I can sort through the ones you've already sent.

I have to tell you more about Steele. There's something below the surface of that man. He's a hard-nosed lawyer. He says he believes in a practical love and quotes scripture to substantiate his view. The man could argue the paint off a wall, but I'm not convinced. I know something's hurt him. Something to do with a sibling. I don't think I told you about his reaction when I suggested that very thing. I thought he was going to crack. Just like the first ice on a pond. Remember the way it crackled and snapped into ragged puzzle pieces? Anyway, that's the sort of reaction I got when I prodded a little too hard with Steele, kind of attacking his negative attitude toward romance. Something has hurt the man real bad. I pray for his emotional healing. <long sigh> I'm not sure *that would take care of his extreme practical nature, however.*

*But back to the banquet. Just a couple more weeks.
Everything is in place. I'm hoping we sell every ticket. I'm
so excited. Wish you could be here in person. I miss you every
day, but I know you're doing an important work.*

*BTW, how are the babies? Starting to grow yet? It still
shocks me to think of someone's abandoning tiny twin girls
by the side of the road. What a miracle they were found in
time and taken to you. I pray for them every day and you,
too, dear friend.*

Lots of hugs and love and prayers,
Hol

Just as she hit SEND, the phone rang. She grabbed the
cordless from the table beside her and answered it.

"Holly, how's my favorite girl?"

"Hi, Nan. How's my favorite grandmother?"

"Right as rain, child. Right as rain."

Holly settled back. A call from Nan always brightened her
day. "You sound cheerful."

"Always am, aren't I?"

Holly chuckled. "You are. But you sound even more
cheerful than usual. What's up?"

"I'm going to visit Missoula."

Holly pushed the laptop to the foot of the lounge chair
and sat up. "It's about time." She'd tried for almost five years
to get her grandmother to revisit the place of her youth, but
she consistently refused, saying she didn't want to ruin her
memories. "Why now, all of a sudden?"

Nan sucked in a breath that sounded quivery and uncertain
to Holly.

"Something isn't wrong, is it?" What if Nan were sick, dying even, and had decided to visit Missoula while she still had the strength?

"Nothing's wrong. In fact, things might be just right."

Holly leaned over her knees, weak with relief. She wasn't ready to lose Nan. She was as close to her as she was to her parents. Nan had been a loving part of Holly's childhood even as she remained a loving force in her life today.

"Holly, I wonder if you aren't going to think me a silly old woman at what I'm going to do."

Holly smiled fondly. "I doubt it."

"You remember I told you what a wonderful time I had in Missoula when I first left home."

"Of course."

"What made it special was a young man I met. He was my first love."

"Grandpa?"

"No, dear. Your grandfather was after that."

Holly did some quick mental adjusting. She'd always assumed the man in the romantic stories was her grandfather. If not— "Then who was this wonderful man, and what happened to him?"

"Nothing. We just went our separate ways. But he phoned me the other day. He lost his wife a year or so ago, and now he wants to see me again. He suggested we meet in Missoula." Nan's voice fell to a whisper. "Where we met in the first place."

"Nan, how exciting. It's like a story."

"You don't think I'm being foolish?"

"It's romantic. They say you never forget your first love."

"Whoever 'they' are." Nan suddenly sounded all grand-motherly. "I'm sure we're different people after fifty years."

"I suppose. What do you plan to do?"

"He didn't say, but I. . ." She paused. "You'll really think I'm a silly old woman now." Again she hesitated, but when she spoke, her voice sounded strong. "I'd like to revisit as many places as possible. Do the things we did back then."

"Oh, Nan. That's so sweet. I don't think you're silly at all. I can help you."

"Holly, I'm scared."

"Nan." Her competent grandmother who had been a widow for twenty years, who changed her own oil, fixed flat tires, and had been known to fire up a chain saw to cut down a tree threatening her house, was afraid? "What's to be scared of?"

"What if I don't feel the same?" Holly strained to hear her words. "What if I do?"

"Don't you think you deserve the chance to find out either way? When are you coming? You'll stay with me, of course."

"Tomorrow. I'm so nervous."

"Don't be. By the way, does this old boyfriend have a name?"

"Henry Davis."

Holly pulled the phone away and stared at it. She must have misunderstood. She put the phone back to her ear. "Would you say that again?"

"Henry Davis, child. He says his grandson is a lawyer in Missoula. You might have heard of him. Steele Davis. Do you know him?"

Holly stared across the balustrade, saw the leaves on the trees, but felt as if she'd leapt off the railing into the wild blue sky.

"Holly, are you still there? Holly?"

"I'm here, Nan. Why didn't you tell me about Henry before?"

"I saw no need."

Holly tried to reconcile this new information with what she knew of Steele. Somehow she couldn't imagine romance in association with a relative of his. "I know Steele Davis. His office is across the street from my café."

"Well, well. Isn't that something? Why haven't you mentioned it?"

Holly laughed. "I didn't see the need."

Nan chuckled. "Seems we both have secrets."

"Nan, I'm not hiding anything." She didn't want Nan to get the wrong idea. "He's just someone I'm working with on the banquet." Nan knew of Holly's desire to raise funds for the orphanage.

"Still, small world."

Holly agreed, and they discussed it a little more then made arrangements for Nan to come to the café the next day. "I'll let Henry know. We can meet there. That way if he turns out to be a scoundrel, you can help me walk away. I hope he isn't. I have such fond memories of our time together."

A few minutes later, they said good-bye. Holly shook her head in wonder and caution. Steele's grandfather of all people. She could well guess Steele's reaction to this, but Holly intended to do what she could to help Nan recreate the summer of her youth. Even if this Henry Davis was at all like his grandson, Nan deserved to enjoy her memories. And if Mr. Davis was a kind old gentleman and treated Nan the way she remembered, then Holly would do everything in her power to help rekindle an old romance.

She lay back and smiled up at the blue sky.

four

The phone rang. Steele's secretary had left already, so he grabbed it.

"Hi, there, young man. How are you doing?" The familiar roar of his grandfather's voice boomed across the airwaves.

"Fine, Grandpops. Are you keeping out of trouble?"

"No fun in that now, is there?"

Steele leaned back and laughed. Pops always bragged about his wild escapades, half fiction, half wishful thinking and maybe—just maybe—a sliver of fact. Like Pops saying he'd caught a raging bull by tossing a rope out the truck window and wrapping the end around the steering wheel column. "Bull tried to charge the truck. Had to keep backing up to keep the grill between me and that red-eyed monster." There might have been a bit of truth in the story. After all, there was a grill the size and strength of a prison gate on the front of the truck Pops used to rattle around on his ranch. "Built tough to stop animals in their tracks," Pops liked to explain. But as to holding the bull single-handedly while driving defensively. . . Well, what could Steele say? It made a good story.

"I'm planning to spend a few days in Missoula."

That explained the call. Pops needed a favor. Not that he'd come right out and ask. He'd let you figure it out yourself. "You can stay with me," Steele said.

"Good. Are you prepared to put up with me for a week or two?"

Steele heard the note of caution in his grandfather's voice, and something else. Excitement maybe. "What are you up to?"

"Thought I'd go girling."

At the idea of his grandfather cruising the streets of Missoula trying to pick up "girls" his age, Steele laughed out loud. "Sure, Pops."

The old man grunted. "Maybe I can show you how it's done, and then you'll get off your duff and find a girl to marry. It's time you gave your father and mother some grandchildren. And me a great-grandchild while I'm still able to recognize him."

Whoa. The old man's slowing down—he used to jump right in there about marriage and kids. Took a whole minute this time.

"Three strapping young men," he'd say about Steele and his brothers. "And not one great-grandchild. Isn't it about time?" He'd look at each of them in turn, studying them like they'd neglected some important duty to the old man.

Good thing Steele and his brothers didn't take offense easily. They simply put it down to his crustiness and laughed it off.

Currently none of them was even married. Steele figured one failed marriage in the family was enough proof that some things were better left alone.

"Really, Grandpops, what's important enough to tear you away from the farm for a week?"

"Maybe two," Pops corrected. "It's kind of a reunion. Don't know if you're aware I spent a summer working in Missoula when I was a kid fresh out of school. Had a good time. Met some nice people. Plan to look some of them up. One in particular I was real fond of and hope to spend time with."

Steele contemplated his grandfather's words, tried to connect them with what he knew about the older man, and felt as if a link or two were missing. "Never knew you worked here. I always think of you on the farm."

"Yes, well, it's been my home forever, it seems. I plan to die here. But I think it could survive my absence for a week or two. You sure you're okay with my company that long?"

"I'm gone most of the day. You'll have the place to yourself." He thought of his grandfather's steadfast habit. "Only one request. No boots in the house."

The man grunted. "You expect me to walk around in my socks? A man could slip and fall doing that."

"Bring some good slippers. When will you be here?"

"Tomorrow. And get set for some serious girling." Pops sounded eager as a young pup released from a leash.

A picture of a wrinkled old woman, half deaf, smelling like liniment as she leered at Pops, brought a burst of laughter from Steele. "I doubt we'd be looking for the same sort of girls."

Pops grunted. "I expect you to find your own girl. I'll just show you how it's done."

Steele still chuckled as they said good-bye. "Girling." He chortled. The pictures flooding his mind would make a great comedy film.

✦

From his office the next morning, Steele watched Holly flitting about with her endless smile, dispensing pink flowers to everyone who sat at one of her tables. No more need to hang about the café. The banquet was organized. He'd succeeded in making sure it didn't turn all lovey-dovey and mushy. They'd have a good substantial meal, fun entertainment, and reasonable decorations. Yes, he'd done his job well. He could relax and let the rest of it fall together.

He stared at the pink flowers in the middle of each occupied table. For some reason just the sight of them made him tense. Maybe it was because they seemed to represent all the things he didn't believe in—romance, living in unrealistic dreams, expecting magic every day of a marriage. The only successful marriages he'd seen were based on something far more solid—shared interests, mutual benefit, a love like the Bible talked about.

He turned back to the papers on his desk. He had appointments and no time to muse over such foolishness.

Several hours later he glanced up again and saw Holly sitting alone at one of the tables, her laptop before her.

She looked toward his office. If he didn't know she couldn't see through the glass, he'd think their gazes had connected. He had a sudden desire for a good, strong cup of coffee and headed across the street.

"Annie," Holly called as she saw him approach. "Bring Steele his coffee." She nodded toward the chair opposite her, waited as if she expected him to have an announcement.

He mentally checked the to-do list for the banquet but couldn't think of anything he'd left undone.

Her expression grew quizzical. "I hear your grandfather is coming to town."

"Grandpops? Yeah. How would you know? You been tapping my phone line?"

She giggled. "As if I'd know how."

He fixed her with a demanding look. "How do you know he's coming?"

She sobered. "My grandmother told me."

He was missing something vital to understanding this conversation. "How would your grandmother know? Does she tap phone lines?"

She frowned in exasperation. "Surely you know they're meeting here this afternoon."

He knew how to keep his face expressionless, how to reveal nothing even when surprised. And her announcement certainly surprised him. Pops wasted no time with his "girling," but how did he start before he was even in town? No wonder he thought Steele and his brothers slow. To Steele's knowledge, none of them had picked up a woman before appearing on the scene.

Holly's expression went from suspicion to impatience. Her eyes grew dark.

Maybe he wasn't hiding his surprise as well as he thought. "He said he was going girling. I thought he was joking."

Her eyes darkened further, as if he'd said something nasty.

"My grandmother told me she and your grandfather were friends more than fifty years ago. In fact, they were boyfriend, girlfriend. Young love, Nan said. Said she'd never forgotten him. He tracked her down through the family she worked for here, and they want to meet again. See if they have that same old feeling."

He choked on a mouthful of coffee.

She jumped up, patted his back, and made soothing noises, though she patted a lot harder than he thought necessary; and when she spoke again, she sounded downright annoyed. "Why does it surprise you? You can't believe they might have enjoyed a little romance when they were young?"

"Pops? My grandpops? You must have the wrong grandfather. He never loved anyone but my grandmother."

She sat down again. Stared at him hard enough that he wondered if she saw his bones beneath his skin. "Nan said she was meeting a man named Henry Davis who was planning to stay with his grandson, Steele Davis, a lawyer in Missoula. Now I ask you, does that sound like someone else's grandfather?"

"No, it doesn't."

"Nan wants to recreate some of the events from back then."

He suddenly leaned forward, his eyes narrowing as he realized what she'd said. What kind of scheme had she and her grandmother cooked up? "She's doing what?"

"They're meeting here. Then they plan to visit some of the places they enjoyed when they were young." She seemed not to notice the way his mouth tightened but forged on with what he could only call belligerence. "Nan says they want to find out if the spark between them is still there. Isn't that cool? I can't think of anything more romantic than rediscovering an old love. Imagine. . .maybe they've loved each other all these years."

"That's disgusting. They both married someone else and raised a family. Besides, it was a half century ago. How can anyone in their right mind think they can turn the clock back?"

Her eyes flared. Dull red stained the tips of her ears. She sat as rigid and straight as the wall beside her. Just when he thought she would explode like an overinflated balloon, she let out a *whoosh* and spoke in slow, measured tones. "Look. I realize this doesn't fit into your view of love and romance."

She had that right.

"But I think they deserve to find out if there's still that spark, as Nan said. I intend to do everything I can to help them."

He snorted. "No doubt you'll give them your most private table and a pink carnation. Or will you give them a little bouquet because it's such a special occasion?" He felt a surge of victory when she ground out a sound of exasperation. He couldn't help a secret smile at the way her eyes flashed daggers.

"Maybe I'll buy them a dozen red roses."

"And give them a card full of sappy love sayings." His harsh tones said what he thought of *that* idea.

She pushed to her feet and lurched to his side. "Sappy? There is nothing sappy about love and romance."

He stilled the desire to put distance between them. "Romance is impractical."

Holly scowled at him.

He didn't much care for the way she breathed hard, curled and uncurled her fists. He stood, exhibiting no rush, though he couldn't wait to escape her presence. Pink flowers and sappy cards? And to think, not too many minutes ago he'd been imagining how pleasant it would be to visit Holly over coffee with no particular agenda between them. "I don't know what your grandmother has in mind, but I won't stand by and see my grandfather become a victim of some scheming woman."

She measured her words out one by one as if squeezing them past an asthma attack. "Make that two scheming women, because I intend to help her all I can."

He gave her a look meant to stop her before she could say anything more.

She ignored his silent warning. "You call yourself a lawyer, yet you ignore the facts. Number one, no one is forcing your grandfather to meet my grandmother. You might ask him who made the first contact. Two, I don't know about your grandfather, but my grandmother is perfectly capable of making her own choices. Nobody will coerce her into doing something she doesn't want to do."

Holly's arguments carried the ring of truth, but Steele didn't care. He had the incredible urge to bang his head against the nearest planter at Holly's blind belief in all this—he glanced around—flowery stuff.

He stalked away. Anger jabbed at him like a hot nail to his heart. Romance was one thing and pink flowers part of it. But turning her romantic notions toward his grandfather, aiding and abetting her desperate grandmother—no way. He would not, could not, in a million years stand by and let those women create a romantic trap to catch his poor grandfather. Sure, the man was strong physically. But he'd lost the love of his life recently. How often had Pops told Steele and his brothers that Grandma had saved him? "She came into my life when I was going through a tough time. I'd had my heart hurt. Thought I'd never be able to love again. Even wondered if life was worth living. Your grandmother changed all that. God bless her."

Maybe his grandfather thought he could replace Grandma and put an end to his mourning. But Pops had to understand it wasn't that easy.

Was Holly's grandmother the woman who'd broken Pops's heart? If so, Steele didn't intend to stand idly by and let it happen again.

How could he stop it? As Holly so angrily pointed out,

their grandparents were capable of making their own choices.

Only one way he could think of to put a monkey wrench in this whole business. He'd stick close to Pops. Run interference on his behalf.

But Pops would not welcome such action.

Steele remembered Pops's invitation to go girling together. It provided the perfect setup. He'd let the old man think he'd taken up the offer. Maybe even let him think he was interested in Holly.

That ought to give him a chance to keep an eye on the proceedings. Holly had a head full of dreams, but Steele had the mind of a lawyer. He'd make sure Pops didn't get swept off his feet—willingly or unwillingly.

He intended to be ready. He canceled his afternoon appointments, shifted his chair so he could look up every minute for a quick study of the café, and pulled out some files to work on. Not that he accomplished anything with his thoughts jumping across the street to the pending meeting.

He saw several older ladies stop for coffee, but none lingered unusually long.

Around four o'clock he watched a slender woman with a floppy red hat stop at the café. Holly hurried out and hugged the woman, nudging the hat askew.

Had to be the scheming grandmother. "The eagle has landed," he muttered. Perfect timing for tea and crumpets. Though he'd never actually met a real-life crumpet.

Holly led the woman to a table.

Steele's eyes narrowed and his jaw clenched as he saw she'd arranged the planters to provide living walls around the table. Subtle? Not Holly. She might as well hang a flashing neon sign—OLD LOVES REKINDLED HERE—proclaiming her intention to see this poor old couple drowning in romance.

Well, not if he had anything to say about it. And he would.

Pops sauntered up, rolling on his cowboy boots with all the swagger of a man fifty years younger.

Steele groaned. Even without seeing his face, he could tell Pops was as eager as a young buck. An easy mark for two women. He'd probably be on one knee before Steele could intervene.

Holly glanced toward his office windows, a silent challenge. She might as well have waved a red flag or slapped him with a leather glove.

With a muttered warning, he charged down the stairs ready to duel.

&

Holly took Nan a cup of rooibos tea. "It's so good to see you. I can hardly wait to share your favorite spots with you." She paused as Nan glanced past her. "Of course you might not be wanting *my* company."

"Nonsense, child. I'm too old to be all—what is it that movie says?—twitterpated about a man."

Holly hid a smile. Nan might believe she was too old to be excited, but she perched on the edge of her chair while her gaze darted past Holly.

Holly knew without turning the moment Mr. Davis stepped into view. Nan froze. Her cheeks stained a dull red. Holly lurched to Nan's side, fearing she would faint. Nan fluttered her hand, her eyes never shifting from the man on the sidewalk.

Slowly Holly turned, prepared to take a good, hard, impartial look at the man who after fifty years had the power to render Nan speechless. There might have been a spark back then, but who knows how the man had changed?

She tried to do a detached assessment. Tall and rangy. A full head of silver hair, eyes as hazel as Steele's. But at the look of wonder and longing and uncertainty in his eyes, Holly lost all ability to be critical. This man adored her nan. Nothing else mattered.

"Mr. Davis." She held out her hand. "I'm Holly Hope, Jean's granddaughter. Please have a chair. What can I bring you?"

The man pulled his gaze toward Holly. He held her hand between his and examined her closely. When he smiled, she felt as if she'd met his favor in some way. "You're very much like your grandmother when I first knew her. You have the same kind smile."

At that moment Holly blessed this man and silently prayed God would grant the older couple renewed love.

Mr. Davis turned his attention back to Nan and slowly crossed to the table. "Jean, I'd have known you anywhere." He took her hand and smiled into her eyes. "You're as beautiful as I remember."

At the look of shy pleasure in Nan's face, Holly pressed her lips together and widened her eyes to keep them from tearing.

The man chuckled as Nan ducked her head. "And just as shy."

Nan laughed. "And you, Henry, are just as full of nonsense as I recall. It's good to see you."

They smiled at each other.

"You going to stand all day or have a seat?" Nan asked.

Mr. Davis laughed heartily. "I see you've added a little vinegar to the mix." He sat in the chair across the tiny table.

"What will you have, Henry? Coffee, tea, or—"

Holly choked back a laugh at the bright color racing up Nan's face.

"You?" Mr. Davis finished. "How about two out of three? I'll have whatever she's having," he said, without taking his gaze off Nan.

Holly hurried to get a pot of tea and put a plate of mixed cookies before the pair. "There you go, Mr. Davis."

Nan smiled up at Holly, her eyes shining like bits of starlight. "Thank you, dear."

Holly winked and squeezed Nan's hand.

"Make it Henry," Mr. Davis said. "This looks delicious. Thank you." But Holly noted he didn't even look at what she'd placed before him.

She slipped away and joined Meggie behind the counter. "Here's hoping no one else comes for a while so they can enjoy some time alone together."

"Uh oh. You spoke too soon." Meggie nodded toward the door.

Steele headed across the street like a steamroller, ready to flatten everything in sight. Halfway across, he slowed, hesitated. If she wasn't mistaken, he sucked in a breath like a spent runner. Then he smiled and continued toward her, slow and easy, as if he had nothing more on his mind than a nice social visit.

Holly knew better. She'd seen the look in his eyes before he masked it. If ever a man was bent on putting an end to romance, Steele was that man. She met him at the edge of the sidewalk. "Come on inside, and I'll get you coffee." She grabbed his elbow and steered him toward the door.

He refused to be steered. "I saw Pops come here." He tried

to edge around the planter blocking his view.

"He and my grandmother are having tea. Let's leave them alone for a few minutes."

He gave her a look of disbelief. "Pops would have a fit if he knew I was here and just ignored him. You're not busy. Why don't you join us?"

"Yes, why don't you two join us instead of muttering out there?" Nan called.

"Steele, get in here. I want to show off my grandson," Henry growled.

Steele grinned at Holly. "Care to say no?"

Holly rolled her eyes. "And incur Nan's wrath? I don't think so." But she didn't care for the gleam in Steele's eyes. He might have won this round, but only by default.

"Me either. Pops can still wield a big stick." He waved her ahead of him.

Meggie, a laugh in her voice, called from inside. "I'll bring you both a coffee."

Steele grabbed two chairs and shoved them up to the table. He sat beside his grandfather. Henry cupped his hand over the back of Steele's neck. "Jean, this is my grandson. His office is right across the street."

Holly felt two pairs of eyes swing from Steele to her, and then the older couple looked at each other, some silent message communicated.

"Jean and I have been talking," Henry said. "I'd like to reintroduce her to Missoula. A lot has changed in half a century."

Holly grinned at the way the older two smiled at each other. She glanced at Steele and saw a speculative look in his eyes. When he saw her watching, he smoothed away the tightness and smiled.

"I expect everything has changed," he said, his voice flat.

Holly wasn't fooled by his relaxed manner. She heard the warning in his voice, knew he had opposition on his mind. She narrowed her eyes and silently informed him she would not let him ruin this reunion. "Anything I can do to help, just ask."

"Actually," Nan said, "we'd like you to join us tomorrow."

"Not a problem." Tomorrow was Sunday, and she didn't open the café on Sundays. She'd enjoy spending part of the day with them if they didn't mind.

"Both of you," Henry added.

Holly met Steele's gaze and felt his tension in the way his smile tightened at the corners, the way his pupils narrowed.

"Sounds like a plan," he said.

A plan? Yeah, right. She could just imagine *his* plan. Did he figure to run interference? How? She jerked her chin just a fraction of an inch. Whatever he planned, she would be there to make sure the day went as Nan and Henry hoped.

"We met at church," Nan said. "We were both at loose ends, so we decided to spend the day together."

"We went on a picnic." Henry chuckled. "Kind of spontaneous. I think we had peanut butter sandwiches."

"I begged some cookies from my employers."

"Wasn't it the pastor who introduced us?"

Nan chuckled. "He probably felt sorry for us alone in the big city."

Henry slapped his thighs. "We want to go to church and then have a picnic. Just like that first day."

Holly sighed. "It sounds so romantic. But you don't need two other people with you."

Nan waved away her protests. "Nonsense. It will be fun to have a couple of young people along, won't it, Henry?"

"Can't think of anything better." He leaned toward Steele and lowered his voice to a gentle rumble. "I just might be able to teach this boy a thing or two."

Steele pushed back in his chair and cast a glance around as if hoping to escape.

Holly had never seen a man look so embarrassed and frightened at the same time, and she couldn't help but laugh.

He shot her a look full of sharp protest and warning.

She covered her mouth and tried to swallow her amusement. Her eyes stung with the effort.

"Pops," he managed to growl, "I don't need your help."

Henry shifted his gaze toward Holly. Her laugh died a sudden death at the look in the old man's eyes.

"Maybe you don't at that. You have a nice little gal here."

Holly gasped. "I'm not—"

Steele laughed. She resisted an urge to toss the rest of her coffee at him and drown the sound. "She's a little shy."

Henry nodded. "Just like her grandmother."

Holly sputtered. "That's not—" How dare Steele let Nan and Henry think there was something between them?

Steele leaned over and patted the back of her hand. "It's okay, Holly. We can go along with the grandparents and enjoy ourselves."

"Yes, dear. I'm sure you can." Nan gave her a warm smile.

Holly sent Steele a look she hoped would burn his mind like a splash of acid, then gave an unconcerned shrug. *Ohh, the man was impossible.*

He leaned back and smiled like a cat full of cream. "Of

course if you're busy, I'm sure we can have fun without you."

As if she'd let him hang around the older couple alone. She could just imagine how he'd throw cold water on any romantic overtures.

"I'm not busy. I'll be glad to go along." Two could play this game. "I can prepare the meal. That is, if you don't object to something a little nicer than peanut butter sandwiches."

Henry gave a roaring laugh. "Little lady, I'd appreciate something a little nicer. How about you, Jean?"

"That would be fine."

"Great." Holly gave Steele a smile full of victory.

He nodded, his answering smile not revealing any hint of defeat.

"We should move along and make way for other customers," Nan said.

"Let me show you downtown Missoula," Steele's grandfather said.

Holly waited until the older couple was out of earshot before she confronted Steele. "I don't know what you're doing letting them assume we're such good friends. But I won't let you ruin this for them."

"Me?" He pressed his hand to his chest as if suffering a sudden pain. "I just want to join in the fun. Why would you think otherwise?"

She could not stop her eyes from squinting and her mouth from puckering. "You want me to believe you're not opposed to a romance between them?"

"Holly, Holly, Holly." He patted her shoulder in a grandfatherly gesture. "Let yourself enjoy the day without all that suspicion. After all, aren't you the purveyor of romance around here? Wouldn't want to ruin that, would we?"

"Ohh. You are up to something. I know it."

He slowly faced her. "I guess that gives me an advantage, because I *do* know what you're up to."

She stared at him. "Me?" His eyes narrowed and turned cold hazel. He suspected—that was crazy. "You really think Nan and I are out to get your grandfather? Open your eyes, Mr. Lawyerman. I don't think your grandfather needs any help from me."

She felt the heat of his anger burning from his eyes. They faced each other, taking measure, assessing the enemy. Suddenly she laughed. "Nope, I don't think he needs any help. It's going to be fun to sit back and watch." She jabbed her finger at him. "Pay attention. You just might learn a thing or two." She laughed again at the fury in his expression.

He jerked around and stalked back to his office.

"Meggie, give me a hand. I have to prepare a picnic for tomorrow." She chuckled. This was going to be a picnic to remember.

five

Steele hurried home earlier than usual. It had taken all of thirty seconds of watching Pops at the café to realize the old man was ready for plucking. Almost begging for it, in fact. Steele's plan to be invited had succeeded. Both grandparents believed he and Holly had more than a passing interest in each other, but unfortunately his plan had its flaws. How could he keep an eye on Pops when he had office hours and commitments? He couldn't. So on to plan B—convince Pops he should forget this whole idea of reviving a fifty-year-old romance.

For some reason that now made no sense, Steele expected Pops to be home waiting for him. He wasn't and didn't show up until almost seven.

Pops grunted when Steele pointed at the cowboy boots. He grabbed a chair and sat down to tug them off then pulled rubber-soled slippers from a bag. "Had to go buy these."

"I saved you some dinner," Steele said, pointing to the congealing chicken and fries.

"I've eaten. And probably a good thing if that's all you have to offer." He shuddered. "Not so good for a man's arteries."

"So I heard."

"You're thirty in a few more months. Time to start taking care of yourself."

Steele tried to remember a single fat-free meal on the ranch and failed. "You still eat half a cow at every meal?"

Pops made a rude noise. "My beef is home-raised. The best you can find."

Steele shrugged and threw the leftovers in the garbage. He couldn't imagine what Pops had being doing since he'd last seen him, but how do you cross-examine your own grandparent? Someone who would as soon wrestle a cow as call your name? And then the old man beat him to the draw.

"You never told me about Holly. You been keeping secrets from an old man? That's not nice, you know."

Steele drew back and studied Pops to see if he was serious. Far as he could tell, he was. Steele shook his head. "You're one to talk. How long have you kept your secret romance hidden? Did Grandma know about Jean?"

Pops slapped his palms down on the counter with a resounding *thwack*. If Steele hadn't known how to keep his face and body under control, he would have cringed. He was almost certain his eyes would have given him away if Pops had cared to notice. He didn't.

"Now listen here, boy. I loved your grandmother. Never cheated on her in thought or deed. She was a good woman. Saved me from myself on more occasions than I care to remember."

"Jean is the woman who left you whipped and broken, isn't she?" He didn't need Pops's answer to know it was true. But perhaps reminding his grandfather would make him see how foolish this whole thing was.

"Boy, we aren't going to discuss things that aren't any of your business."

"Maybe I'm making it my business to see you don't buy yourself a heap of trouble. What makes you think it won't happen again?"

Pops grunted. "Seems I'm old enough to take care of myself."

"What is it you always say? 'No fool like an old fool'?"

"If you're suggesting I'm making a fool of myself—" Suddenly Pops chuckled. "Maybe I am at that. And I'm here to tell you, I don't mind a bit. Sometimes, young man, you need to give your emotions some freedom." He squinted hard at Steele.

Steele groaned. Here it came. The lecture on how he needed to get off his duff and charm some little gal into marrying him. Before Pops could deliver the message, Steele defended himself. "I don't intend to ever let my emotions rule my head."

"Well, then, there's your trouble. But I see the way you look at little Holly. Might be she's just the one to make you forget all your hard-and-fast rules."

Steele stuffed back his frustration. The old man was beyond reasoning with, which made it all the more necessary for Steele to run interference. Back to plan A. "Yeah, Pops. You could be right." Let Pops think Holly held an alluring interest for Steele. That way he could hope to be included in their outings, at least the evening ones—and wouldn't that be when all the lovey-dovey stuff took place? He'd just keep an eye on Pops and those two women. Make sure their feet remained on the ground as firmly as his own. Pops would explode like one of his angry bulls if he knew Steele intended to see this little holiday didn't turn into déjà vu all over again. Steele didn't intend to tell him.

Pops perched on one of the stools and leaned both elbows on the counter. "Now tell me about Holly. She seems like a nice girl. I can see, though, that you need some help in wooing her. My guess is she's the kind of gal that likes to be made to feel special."

Let Pops think he could help Steele, but frustration rose in his throat. This plan was going to prove a real challenge.

&

Steele followed his grandfather into the pew. The old man slipped past Holly and sat on the other side beside Jean. That left Steele to sit beside Holly. Pops was anything but subtle, but not a problem. Let Pops think, let them all think, he joined them because he embraced this romantic stuff.

Holly glowed with some sort of inner excitement. She stole glances at him out of the corner of her eye, each time her eyes flashing light.

It made his skin itch. He rubbed his chin. She was up to something. He wished he knew what. Not that it mattered. He had his own agenda—to see that four pairs of feet remained planted in reality.

He'd sat close to her a few times in the past weeks as they worked on the banquet. He knew she didn't have the best singing voice in the world, but what she lacked in quality she made up for with enthusiasm. He admired that.

He settled back when the singing ended and the sermon began. He normally enjoyed this respite from the daily pressure of his work. Today was no different. Pastor Don challenged them all to reject competition with one another and seek to promote the peace of Christ. Steele applied it to factions based on denominational differences. No way did it have anything to do with this unspoken feud between him and Holly. Hardly a feud even. Just a slight dissimilarity in viewpoints. Besides, his motive was right. He only wanted to protect Pops.

It bothered him a tiny bit that he was misleading Pops about his interest in Holly. Not that she wasn't a nice enough young woman. Except for her sentimental belief in romance and flowers and—

A vision of pink flowers in a lattice-topped planter filled his mind. His insides twisted and knotted like the tea towels he'd pulled from the dryer last night. What was it with pink flowers? He dismissed the errant thought and concentrated on the closing remarks.

After the service, the four of them gathered on the sidewalk.

"Where is this picnic to take place?" Steele demanded.

"Down by the river," Holly answered as the other two wandered away. "The lunch is ready at the café. We can go that way."

"A walk. How nice." He put false enthusiasm into his voice and received a startled look from Holly.

She studied him a minute, as if wondering how sincere he was, then gave a quirk of her eyebrows, silently informing him she would accept his gesture as sincere as long as he lived up to it.

"Authentic," she said. "That's how Nan and Henry did it the first time."

He made sure she noticed how he rolled his eyes in disbelief. "We're going to have a little trouble making the river walk look like it did fifty years ago."

"Doesn't matter. Come on." She tucked her hand through his arm and headed him down the sidewalk.

What was with that? Was she trying to keep him away from Pops? But the older couple followed.

Holly's hand was warm and soft. He thought of sunshine and flowers—white ones, red ones, any color but pink.

He would not think pink. As a lawyer, he knew he should question that idea, but instead he pushed it away.

They stopped to pick up a cooler and a big wicker basket at J'ava Moi.

"Couldn't you have given us each a brown bag?" he murmured as he hefted the cooler to his shoulder.

She smiled sweetly. "Wouldn't want to give the grandparents food poisoning now, would I?"

"So this chest is full of food on ice. And the basket?"

"Need dishes, don't we?"

"Not for sandwiches."

"We're going to have to hurry to catch up." Pops and Jean had gone ahead.

Steele waited for her to lock the café, then they strode after the older couple. But it was impossible to hurry with the awkward basket banging at Holly's shins.

He shifted the cooler to his other shoulder and grabbed the handle of the basket. "Give me that. We'll never catch them."

His hand brushed hers. Again he thought sunshine and flowers. This time he didn't picture any pink flowers, just pots of sweet purple ones, and found, to his surprise, he liked purple flowers. He grunted. *Steele, give your head a shake.* Sunday was no excuse to leave his brain in park. He stared at her hand as she refused to release the handle. "Come on, Holly. Be reasonable."

"Let's both carry it."

Let's not.

She took a step.

What could he do but grasp the basket between them, feeling the connection between their hands? Of course he felt a connection. After all, their fingers rubbed together. It would have been far more surprising if he hadn't felt it. Would have signaled his hand was numb or paralyzed. Nope. Wasn't his hand that was the problem—it was his brain. It was numb. He should have grabbed a coffee somewhere to jump-start it.

Trouble was, the connection had nothing to do with the touch of her hand. It had everything to do with the sweet, crazy, mixed-up feeling he got around her. That strange yearning hollowness, or hunger, a longing—whatever it was—that grew more familiar each time they were together.

Pops would laugh himself sick if he knew how Steele was thinking. But no way would the old man find out, because as of this minute, Steele put an end to his mental detour.

They caught up to Pops and Jean as they reached Caras Park. Jean stopped and pressed her hand to her chest. "Oh, my. This is much different." She tilted her head. "Do I hear 'Battle Hymn of the Republic'?"

"That's the carousel," Pops said, leading Jean in that direction.

Steele's stomach rumbled. His neck fired off a protest at the weight of the cooler on his shoulder. "Let's find a picnic table first." They found one close to a bunch of trees, next to the river walk. Wildflowers trailed along the pathway. The river tumbled past.

Holly opened the basket and pulled out a white cloth. She flipped it over the table.

Steele's stomach ached from hunger. Pops had insisted on a light breakfast of fruit and yogurt. A man could starve on such fare.

Holly lifted out four white china plates and silverware.

Silverware? Real, shiny silverware? This was a picnic not a banquet. Though he'd welcome banquet food. He'd imagined sandwiches, but now he pictured slabs of ham on the plates, mounds of potato and macaroni salads, and fresh buns slathered with butter. He swallowed hard. "Can I help?"

She put stemmed goblets at each place. "You can pour the drinks." She handed him a long-necked bottle of sparkling apple juice.

He shook his head as he unwrapped the lid, screwed it off, and filled the goblets. No need to wonder what Holly's plans were for the day—romance at its best, or worst, but Pops didn't need any encouragement. "I thought the idea was to recreate the events of yesteryear. Wouldn't water have been more appropriate?"

Holly only laughed. "I bet they wished they had something special back then, so why not give it to them now?"

He had lots of reasons. Reality, practicality, safety, protecting Pops. But Jean and Pops, who had gone to the pathway to look out on the river, saw the table set and hurried back before he could give her even one bit of rationale.

"Holly, this is beautiful. Makes me feel special." Nan hugged her granddaughter. "Thank you."

Pops grinned like a silly pup. "Looks a lot better than our first picnic."

"I guess it's not the same," Steele said. *Nothing's the same—can't you all see that?* It was silly to think they could bring back the past.

"It's better. Lots of things about the present are better than the past." Pops smiled at Jean as he spoke.

Steele clenched down on his jaw so hard it would take

concerted effort to release it. Pops was so vulnerable. So eager to be hurt again.

Jean looked starry-eyed and mellow. But Steele wasn't ready to believe this whole business was above suspicion.

"Did you bring your camera?" Jean asked Holly. "Can you take a picture of us? I always wished I had some pictures of that summer."

"Hang on a minute." Holly pulled a foil-covered bundle from the basket and unwrapped it to reveal a plant covered in pink flowers.

Steele's jaw tightened even more. He couldn't tear his gaze from the pink as a churn of emotions flooded through him, staining every thought, burning away everything but the taste of anger. He hated pink flowers. He didn't realize he'd spoken the words aloud until he felt three people stare at him in surprise.

"Boy," Pops said, "that's downright rude of you. Holly, they're beautiful."

Steele closed his eyes and tried to blot from his mind the sight of those flowers. He sucked in sanity, glanced at Holly. Her eager expression no longer existed. Instead she looked hurt, offended. She blinked rapidly, as if the wind had blown something into her eyes. His insides gave another vicious twist. "It's nothing personal, Holly. I'm sorry I said anything."

Holly nodded, but her smile seemed stiff and unnatural. "Apology accepted." She ducked her head and refused to look at him.

He could hardly blame her. Even though it wasn't anything to do with her, he understood he'd managed to attack something near and dear to her. He hadn't meant to hurt her and didn't care for the way it made him feel all prunelike inside. Somehow he had to make it up to her.

He headed in her direction intending to—

Pops pulled Jean to his side. "Now take our picture."

Holly turned on her camera and took a couple of exposures.

Steele stopped, filled with confusion at the sight of Pops and Jean with their arms around each other, smiling into each other's faces with such—

Steele shook his head. They were old friends, enjoying memories of the past. There could be nothing more. They'd both married others, raised families, lived whole lives without once seeing each other. No way could they fall in love so easily. Unless they were desperate. Which was not a good way to be around love.

And Holly smiling and encouraging them? He wanted to put an end to this whole scene. No. He wanted to be part of it instead of outside it. How could he want such differing things at the same time? What was going on inside his head? Whatever it was felt unfamiliar and scary. He needed to eat before his brain grew any fuzzier. But everyone else seemed more interested in pictures.

"This one is perfect." Holly handed the camera to Jean.

Jean blushed to the roots of her hair. "I look like a star-struck kid."

"You're beautiful when you blush," Pops said. "I remember that about you."

"Oh, you." She fluttered her hands and turned to Holly. "Now you and Steele."

All Steele's efforts to get his thoughts squared away failed. He backed up. He could not be part of this. . . this. . .

Holly shook her head. "Uh uh. This is *your* picnic."

"Come on, boy. Get over here," Pops roared.

No way did Steele want to pose behind that bunch of pink flowers. He looked at Holly and saw a reflection of his horror. He blinked. What did she have to be so antagonistic about? Apart from the pink-flower comment, he'd been nothing but charming. She must have a problem of some sort that had nothing to do with him.

Her resistance made him change his mind. He could handle this. It was only a posed picture. It meant nothing. "Sure, why not?" He took a step toward the table, focused on the pink flowers, and paused.

"Oh, give it up." Holly plucked the plant off the table and set it on the ground. "Just for this picture—then it goes back."

She showed Jean how to use the camera then joined him behind the table.

Pops groaned. "Show a little affection. Put your arm around her. Stop looking like you've got a toothache. Come on, Holly. Show him how much you care."

Holly laughed. "Yes, Henry." And she put her arm around Steele's waist and pinched him.

He jumped. "Hey." He glowered down at her.

She smiled up as sweet as honey on morning toast. "Smile, Steele." She dropped her voice to a low whisper. "Even if it kills you, or I'll pinch you again. You are not going to ruin Nan's special day with hating pink flowers and grumbling about everything nice."

He bared his teeth. "How's this?"

"Most attractive." She smiled toward her grandmother.

"All done," Jean announced. "Want to see?"

Holly glanced at the picture so quickly he knew she couldn't have seen it.

He did the same. "Can we eat now? I'm starved."

"I'll get right at it." She put the flowers back on the table and opened the cooler.

He wasn't fooled by the false cheerfulness of her voice. Beneath the polite words, he heard anger. Well, he was doing his best. She should at least give him credit for trying.

She pulled out a tray of finger food—tiny cubes of cheese on toothpicks, grape-sized tomatoes, slices of cucumber, baby carrots, and coils of deli meat.

His hunger grabbed at his gut. He could clean off that whole tray and not fill a quarter of his empty stomach. He waited for the good stuff.

Out came a plastic-covered silver plate with tiny little sandwiches—crusts cut off, cookie-cutter, fancy shapes.

There had to be more to eat than that, or he would starve.

Another plate. This one piled high with a tower of little tarts with some sort of yellowish brown filling. "What are those?" He hadn't meant to sound so harsh, but he was desperately hungry.

"Individual quiches." She shot him a venomous look. "And don't bother telling me real men don't eat quiche."

"Never crossed my mind." He wondered what she'd say if he ate the entire stack. He watched and waited for her to pull out more food—the good stuff. The real stuff.

She waved at the grandparents, who had gone to look at some of the flowers.

That was it? He looked longingly toward the street, knowing fast food was only a few blocks away. Knowing if he went for it, Pops would skin him alive and nail his hide to the outside of his barn. Pops had threatened to do so many times in the past. Steele had never doubted he could do it. He no longer thought he would, but a wise man never played with fire.

He hid a sudden grin. He could imagine Pops's reaction to this fine fare. "A man has to eat something substantial if he expects to handle a good day of work." Maybe Pops would end the meal with a trip to one of the fast-food places. Steele considered which ones were closest. His vehicle was back at the church. He could jog back for it and return in less than fifteen minutes. Right now he didn't care where they went so long as he got some real food.

Pops and Jean sat side by side, leaving Steele to sit beside Holly. Pops held out his hands. "Let's pray."

Steele bowed his head and concentrated on Pops's big, work-rough hand on one side and tried not to think of how Holly's small, cool hand on the other side sent a queer mingling of anger and longing through him. If he wasn't starving, he'd be able to think better. He wouldn't have this confusion. He never heard a word of his grandfather's grace and only realized "amen" had been said when Pops dropped his hand.

He forced himself to release Holly's hand when she tugged.

"I wish I could have done something this special that first day," Pops said as he checked out the picnic fare.

Yeah, right. They would have starved to death, and then he, Steele, would have a different grandfather. Or maybe never been born.

Jean chuckled. "I don't remember caring what we ate. It was just nice to have someone to share a day off with." She helped herself to the finger food as Holly passed it.

"I know Nan had a job as a nanny, but what brought you

to Missoula?" Holly asked Pops as she shuffled the trays in his direction.

Steele restrained himself from grabbing the food and stuffing his mouth. When the trays finally reached him, he took half of what was left, knowing he'd still be hungry when it was gone. He wrapped cucumber and tomatoes in the meat as Pops answered Holly's question.

"I grew up on a ranch an hour away. A struggling, dirt-poor ranch where a man—or a boy—could work from daylight to dark and never catch up. Where about all you got as reward for the hard labor was more of the same. My father and I had words. I came to Missoula to earn some money and gain some freedom. I was pretty good with motors and found a job in a garage. I thought I had it made."

His mouth full of food, Steele stared at Pops. A dirt-poor ranch? He chewed enough to get the vegetables down. "The ranch isn't poor."

"Not now. I've put in fifty years getting it where it is. But back then—" He shrugged.

"What took you back to the ranch?" Holly asked.

Steele watched Jean, her fork poised halfway to her mouth. He had the feeling she wanted to know Pops's answer more than Holly.

"My father was injured. I knew if I didn't go back home, the ranch would be gone."

Jean lowered her fork to her plate. "I always wondered what happened. Why didn't you tell me?"

Pops toyed with the food before him. "I couldn't face you again. I had nothing to offer you."

"Don't you think I should have had a chance to decide that?"

Pops sent Steele and Holly an apologetic look then turned to take Jean's hands. "Jean, you had such big dreams. You planned to get a nanny job in Europe and see the world. I faced nothing but hard work and poor wages."

Nan patted Pops's cheek. "I was hurt that you left without a word. I always figured you'd found someone you preferred and didn't know how to tell me."

"Nothing like that."

The four of them turned back to the food. Steele ate half a dozen of the little sandwiches, finding them full of some sort of tasty filling. He didn't dare ask what it was. And the quiches? Whoever said real men didn't eat quiche had not tasted Holly's. After Jean and Pops had both declined any more, Steele eyed the remaining stack.

"Help yourself," Holly invited, correctly interpreting his hungry look.

Eight quiches later, he discovered the hollowness of hunger had disappeared.

She reached into the cooler and pulled out a tray of fresh fruit, more cheese, and a plate stacked with muffins. Then she pulled thermos bottles of coffee from the picnic basket.

"Nan, did you meet Grandfather after Henry left?" Holly asked.

"No, dear. I actually went home a few weeks later." She smiled gently at Pops. "It wasn't the same anymore." She turned back to Holly. "Your grandfather was an old friend. We just seemed to fit together after that. He was good to me. I've missed him these past twenty years."

Holly turned to Henry. "And your wife? How did you meet her?"

"She came to care for an elderly lady in the community.

At the time I was kind of a mess. Fighting hard to satisfy my father, trying to keep the ranch from disaster. Alma was sweet and kind and understanding. She pointed me back to trusting God."

Steele figured it was time they all stopped flirting with the allure of this whole setup and got back to trusting God before Pops ended up in another emotional mess. But right now he was too busy enjoying his coffee and the satisfaction of a good feed to think of how to express his thoughts without inviting further wrath from the old man.

six

Holly sighed her satisfaction that both Nan and Henry had enjoyed their long years of marriage. She sighed again at the sorrow of their lost first love.

Nan seemed to read her thoughts and reached over to pat her hand. "We were just kids. I don't suppose either of us knew what we wanted."

Henry nodded. "I felt obligated to help my father. I knew the ranch was at risk. Didn't see how I could possibly ask a woman to give up her dreams to share nothing, and that's all I had."

"I know what I want." Holly was a few years older than Nan would have been at the time, but her dreams of a magical love to last forever hadn't changed since she was a small child.

Nan smiled gently. "You might discover your wants change when you're faced with reality. I know mine did. All my fine dreams of travel didn't mean a thing when I was so lonely my heart hurt."

"I'm glad you found someone to fill that loneliness." Henry pushed to his feet. "Shall we clean up then wander around a bit?"

Holly waved them away. "You show Nan the sights while Steele and I put stuff away."

"We'll do that." Henry took Nan's arm, and they headed toward the carousel.

Steele grunted and stared after them.

"I think they've found love again," Holly said.

"Or maybe they're so lonely they'll jump at any chance to share their lives with someone."

"No. I think they loved each other when they were kids. They lost that or maybe walked away from it. They've spent most of their lives loving someone else, but now they've found each other again and rediscovered the love of their youth." One look at his face and she knew he didn't believe it. "And if it's simply loneliness, what would be so wrong with that?"

"Nothing as long as they both understand the game rules." He pointed at the remains of the picnic. "Either way, isn't this romantic setup just a little too blatant?"

"What's with you and pink flowers?"

"I just don't like them."

"So you said. Why?"

"Does there have to be a reason?"

"It seems odd to hate them just because they're pink."

He stared at the flowers and shuddered.

She'd guess he didn't know how his eyes had grown stark. Something had caused this reaction to the flowers even if he didn't care to admit it. She'd be willing to put his dislike of romantic "trappings" down to the same cause. "Maybe you should get counseling."

He bolted to his feet. "If that isn't the stupidest thing I've heard in a long time. Just because I don't like pink flowers, you think I'm crazy."

She shrugged. "No one said you were crazy, but you have to admit it's a weird hang-up. And closely connected to your fear of romantic things, I'm guessing."

"Wow. No need for me to see a shrink. I'll just consult Miss Holly Hopes-for-the-Best. Funny you don't see any association between the divorces I witness in my office and my caution about candlelight and flowers. You want to see a long-lasting marriage—you give me a couple with common interests, shared ideals, even a business arrangement."

She nodded occasionally as she piled up the used dishes and stowed everything away. She wrapped the pink flowers in foil and put them in the basket. "They're gone. Do you feel better?"

"No. Yes."

She laughed, earning her a black look from the confused lawyer. "Steele, I think our grandparents are going to prove you wrong about romantic love." She turned to watch them. Henry bent and plucked a flower and tucked it behind Nan's ear. "Isn't that sweet?"

She didn't have to look at Steele to know his face would be thunderous.

"What my grandfather didn't tell you—" Steele's voice grated with disapproval. "He turned into an angry, bitter young man after he left Missoula. I don't know how many times I heard him credit my grandmother with saving him from destruction. He gave her flowers for every special occasion and for no reason whatsoever. My mom always said it was a waste of good money. She figured he could have had a fortune to invest by the end of each year with what he spent on them."

"This is your mother—your father's business partner?" She dripped sarcasm from every word. No doubt he could have reached out and scooped up handfuls of it. Of course, all sorts of marriages worked, but his parents' sounded cold as the inside of a fridge.

"Yes. And I might point out they've been married almost thirty-two years. Happily."

"That's nice. It's no doubt where you learned romance has no place in a relationship."

"I'm sure it's nothing to do with what I see in my office."

"Oh, wait. There was something about a sibling, wasn't there?"

He grabbed the tablecloth and folded it precisely. He handed it to her to put in the basket. "Any coffee left?"

"Subject closed. Got it. A pink flower phobia and a taboo subject. Interesting dynamics going on here." She refilled his cup with some of her fine Arabica coffee, poured a little more into her own, and sat down.

He glowered at her a minute then sat beside her. "Everything seems to be in order for the banquet."

"Yup. Looking good. Unless something comes up, we don't have anything to do until that weekend. I've put up a poster for helpers to set up."

"Lots of takers, I suppose. Like the hoards that wanted to serve on the planning committee."

His wry humor tickled her. She laughed and placed a playful punch on his shoulder. "You and I did fine together, didn't we?"

The look he gave her made her laugh again.

"Surprised, aren't you?"

He blinked and then laughed. "Yeah, I guess I am at that. We not only did fine, but it was kind of fun. At times."

"Ohh." She pressed her palm to her chest in mock gratitude. "Faint praise from the practical lawyer. I can't believe it."

He shifted his gaze away then returned it to her, his eyes

light green, a slightly embarrassed look pulling at the corners of his mouth. "I'm having trouble believing it myself."

She looked at him with eyes that saw him with new insight, to a hurting heart, a doubting mind, and other things too fragile and new to name. She felt him studying her with the same intensity, wondered what he saw as his gaze probed past the outside layer she presented to the public. His eyes darkened; his gaze reached toward her soul. She held her breath, waited for his approval, waited. . .

A tune intruded. She blinked and turned to locate her cell phone in the basket. "It's Mom. I'd better take the call. Sorry." She hit the TALK button. Sorry to lose the moment before she knew his response; disappointed because she'd hoped for his approval. She knew something was wrong with that thought, but before she could examine it, she said, "Hello, Mom."

"Hi. What are you doing?"

"Mom, you wouldn't believe it. I just had a picnic with Nan and a man she knew fifty years ago. It's so romantic." She turned her back to Steele so she didn't have to bear the desperate way he rolled his eyes and pretended to gag. She told her mother all about it, enjoyed her mother's excited response, then asked, "How are you guys doing?"

"Great. We have a honeymoon couple coming tonight and a famous actor on Monday."

"Oh, fun. Where's Dad?"

"Making sure the flowers and lawn are perfect."

She ended the call a few minutes later. "My mom. She and Dad own a resort in the Kalispell area. They often have famous guests." She named the actor who had booked. "And honeymooners. Mom likes to go all out for them."

Steele looked bored. "Let me guess. This is where you get all your ideas about romance." He sighed. "I know the track record on actors' marriages isn't good. It would be interesting to see how many of your 'honeymooners' are still together a year or two later."

She waved her hand at him. "Don't knock romance. Despite your doubts, it usually works."

He met her look again. She felt the same deep-throated tug. And then he gave a brisk nod, and the moment disappeared. "I have no interest in a relationship based on such nonsense. I hope to marry someday, but it will be because of mutual, practical interests."

Holly jerked her gaze away and prayed he hadn't seen the disappointment flashing through her. She immediately scolded herself. Sure, she and Steele enjoyed planning the banquet together more than either of them had anticipated. Sure, she enjoyed his ironic sense of humor and liked the open affection between him and Henry. None of that provided reason for wishing he could be more romantic. And she had no interest in a "practical" relationship.

❧

For the next few days, Holly saw little of Nan and even less of Henry as they spent their days exploring the city. Nan fell into bed exhausted so early every evening Holly barely had time to discover what the couple had done. As for Steele, he had all but disappeared. Of course, they had no need to meet. The banquet required nothing more of them for now, the grandparents kept busy, and Holly had to work. As did Steele. She caught glimpses of him entering the building across the street.

She sighed. Why should she feel so lonely? Nothing had

changed. With a start, she realized something had—she had. Like it or not, she'd gotten used to Steele running over for coffee once or twice a day. She missed his company, which was as corny as an old country-and-western song. All they did when they were together was argue.

Yes, she missed him even though she kept busy serving guests, giving them pink flowers and hand-painted cards.

She looked at the cart, with many of the flowers already dispensed. What could have happened to Steele to make him hate pink flowers?

At the sound of approaching footsteps, she turned. "Steele." She stopped at the husky sound of her voice, took a deep breath, and tried again. "Hi." Still a little airy but not too revealing, she hoped. Like what was she afraid to reveal—surprise, pleasure? Yes, both.

"Annie," she called into the shop. "Could you bring an espresso for Steele and a mocha for me, please?"

They headed toward the table against the window. She'd taken to putting the planter full of purple pansies next to this table.

"How have you been?" she asked.

"Good. Busy."

They made a few more conversational comments. She wondered if he'd come for a particular reason, or had he missed their visits?

He bent over the purple blossoms. "They smell good."

Her insides felt like a drink of sweet coffee at his appreciation of the flowers. She was glad she had moved them here and shifted the pink ones away.

"I love their scent." She leaned over and breathed deeply of the dark pansies.

What was she thinking? Her face was inches from Steele's. She was certain the blaze of her embarrassment lit her face as if she'd hidden votive candles in her cheeks. She pulled back slowly, grasped the cup Annie placed before her, and studied the contents. She lifted the cup to her mouth then set it back without taking a drink. No way could she swallow. Her throat constricted as though it were being squeezed by a fist.

He sat up straight. Took a drink. Shifted. Rolled his head as if his neck hurt.

She cleared her throat with a little cough. "You don't mind purple flowers?"

"No. I know. It's strange. I should see a shrink."

She couldn't tell if he meant to be cross with her for her suggestion, so she stole a glance at him.

He grinned. "Of course, it might be cheaper simply to avoid pink flowers."

At the teasing look in his eyes, her throat closed again. For a minute she thought she might suffocate as she struggled to suck in air. She'd always known he was handsome, with dark blond hair that dipped over his forehead in a beguiling wave, a strong chin with the slightest hint of a dimple in the center, and eyes she'd admired from first glance. But she'd never before felt the full potency of his look.

Her eyes stung with a queasy mingle of embarrassment and acute awareness. She shifted away, instantly regretted breaking the contact, and reversed her gaze.

"Marty and the Mice canceled," he said.

The real reason for his visit? Why should she be so disappointed? She wasn't. If anything, it was a relief to be released from her dreadful awareness.

"Marty and the Mice?" She chuckled. "I was so looking

forward to the explanation behind that name for a band. We had a couple of bands we turned down when we decided to limit it to four. Can one of them fill in at the last minute?"

"I'll call and see. It would be nice to have the four since we have it set up for that."

"Good thing we didn't print the programs."

"My idea, as I recall."

"Yes, Mr. Practical. You were right on this one."

He quirked one eyebrow as if to suggest he'd been right more often than that if she cared to notice.

"Okay, you've been right a couple of times."

"All right then." He grinned at her, and she told herself it was foolish to feel so pleased. "I'm liking this. Care to be more specific?"

"Let me think." She tilted her chin as if giving it serious thought. "No."

She put the brakes on silly emotions. "I suppose we should finalize the judging forms." They had agreed to eliminate the bands by means of judges rather than the audience.

"We had several criteria—audience appreciation, creativity of presentation, musical ability. Anything else?"

"It's all about having fun. Only thing I might suggest is to rate the criteria in order of importance."

He chuckled. "Like audience appreciation is more important than musical ability."

"Exactly. So let's make sure the judges know that."

"We could weigh each point differently."

"Huh?"

"Sure. Audience appreciation has a value of, say, ten, and the judges rate it one to ten. Creativity in presentation, a value of eight; musical ability, five. So a band that is a real crowd pleaser could get a ten, an eight, and maybe a two for ability."

"Steele, I hate to admit it, but that's a real good idea."

He sat up straighter and looked pleased with himself. "Practical has its up side."

"Yeah. I guess so." She thought of the presentation she and Heather had prepared. "Heather has been so helpful with the slide show. It's really a portrait of her work over there."

"I'm glad it's going well. I'm sure you and Heather have done a good job. It was a great idea." He held his thumb up in a salute of approval. His smile filled his eyes with such kindness she ached inside.

They talked some more about the upcoming banquet, laughing at the names the bands had given themselves.

"I'm excited about the whole thing," she said. "My prayer is that it goes so well we raise enough money for the new roof."

"Let's join our prayers in asking for that." He reached for her hands across the table.

They'd prayed for the success of the banquet in the past, but never before had she felt such unity of purpose. She let him take her hands and focused her thoughts on the purpose of the banquet—the orphans in Africa.

Steele prayed. "Heavenly Father, God of all mercy and grace, the giver of good gifts, we ask You to touch this banquet and the entertainment with Your power and blessing so, in turn, the little kids in Africa might be blessed and especially that they might learn of Your love through our gifts." He stopped.

Holly wanted to pray out loud, too, but fought to squeeze

words past the thickness in her brain—part gratitude, part surprise, and complete confusion. This was Steele Davis, she informed her muddled brain. Logical, practical, scared to death of pink flowers and romance—not the kind of man she should be feeling so confused about.

She sucked in air, laden with the scent of purple pansies and espresso coffee, and forced her throat to work. "Dear Lord, help things to go so well our expectations will be exceeded. Help Heather as she cares for so many children, so many needs. May we be able to provide the funds to fix the roof before next rainy season. Thank You. Amen."

Steele squeezed her fingers gently. "It's in God's very capable hands."

All her serious self-talk vanished like an e-mail lost in cyberspace at the way he looked so content and sure of God's control. It gave her a dizzying sense of something so good and strong and attractive about him. She gently extracted her hands before she totally lost her equilibrium. "Care for another coffee?"

He studied his empty cup as he seemed to consider the question.

Of course, he would have appointments. He didn't have time to linger over coffee any more than she did. But, surprisingly, only two customers had shown up in a half hour or more, and they had opted to sit inside. Annie had no trouble coping with their needs. Holly shifted, prepared to retract her offer, plead work.

"Sure, I could use another."

"Annie, refills, please," Holly called.

Suddenly she could think of nothing to say to this man. Which was stupid, considering they each had a grandparent on the loose. "So what are the grandparents up to? Nan falls into bed practically as soon as she gets home."

"Pops does the same. When I ask what he's been doing, he says walking and talking or having coffee and talking. I think they've gone to the museum and a couple of galleries."

"I hope Nan isn't wearing herself out. Mom and Dad would hold me personally responsible if she made herself sick."

"Has she said anything about what she and Pops are talking about?"

Holly sat back and studied Steele, saw the glint of determination in his eyes. "If I said they were talking marriage, would you try to dissuade them?"

His gaze grew darker, harder. "I might."

She laughed. "Then it's a good thing I'm not going to say that."

He leaned forward, his look so intense she squirmed and tried to look away. "Because you don't want me to know or because Jean hasn't said anything?"

She stuck out her chin. He didn't intimidate her. At least not very much. "Yes."

He scowled. "Yes what?"

"Yes, sir?"

He laughed. "You forgot to salute."

"Oh, yeah. Sorry." She touched two fingers to her forehead. "Sir."

"Do I get the feeling you won't tell me if you don't want to?"

"Yup. You got it."

"You can't blame me for worrying about Pops. He's—"

"Vulnerable. I know. You've said it before." She suddenly felt sorry for the concern in his eyes. "But Nan hasn't said anything to me. She's come back a few times looking a little troubled. I'm not sure what that's all about." She leaned forward and tapped her finger on the table directly in front of Steele. "I don't want to see Nan hurt, either."

He searched her eyes as if looking for something.

She held his gaze, letting him see and feel the slight shift of dynamics between them. She couldn't say exactly what it meant, didn't want to think about it too deeply at this time. She only knew the change felt good and right and scary and dangerous.

He smiled. "Does that mean romance isn't necessarily the answer for our grandparents?"

She laughed. "Romance is not the problem. It's a good way to explore relationships. It satisfies the need for affirmation in each of us. But I admit there has to be more than that. I want Nan to be romanced, but I also want her to be comfortable with the realities of a relationship with your grandfather."

He leaned back, held up his thumb in another salute. "Right on." Suddenly he jerked forward, grabbed her hands, and gave her a look so intense it made her eyes water. "Tell me, Holly Hope, have I had any influence in making you admit the need for practicality?"

She tore her gaze from his, studied their united hands, wondered at the myriad of emotions springing from that simple touch—amusement, hope, affirmation.

Affirmation? He was no romantic, but there was something solid about him that felt good and right.

She pulled her thoughts back to his question. "I'm not saying anything."

He chuckled. "On the grounds it might incriminate you?"

She tried unsuccessfully to stop her laugh from escaping. "Something like that."

"So we both agree we need to make sure our grandparents keep their feet firmly on the ground? I've been thinking it's time I encourage Pops to go back to the ranch. Put an end to this romantic foray. Why don't you see if you can convince Jean to go home?"

She jerked back. "I will do no such thing. I don't want Nan hurt, but I am fully behind her if she wants to pursue her interest in Henry. No way would I do anything to come between them. That's their decision to make." She huffed hard, mad at herself as much as at Steele. How could she even think he'd changed or things between them had changed? He was as stubborn, as practical to the point of cruelness, as unappealing as ever. And if she felt just a twinge of regret at having to admit she'd hoped otherwise, she could blame no one but herself and her eternal romantic optimism.

"I will help my grandmother any way I can. They both deserve the chance to recreate this special time from their youth, and if it leads to something in their declining years, I'll be thrilled."

Steele pushed back and got to his feet. "I see you aren't prepared to be reasonable about this. The way I see it, Pops is too vulnerable. He needs someone to run interference, make sure he thinks with his head and not his heart. Your grandmother has had twenty years to plan this. Pops—"

She jumped to her feet, fighting an incredible urge to do the man bodily harm. It didn't bother her a bit that he outweighed her by fifty pounds or more and his lean body showed the effects of all the time he spent in physical activity. "Stop right there." She pressed her fingertip to his chest. "If you accuse my grandmother of scheming, I won't be responsible for what I do."

His eyes flashed that pale color again. And then he laughed. "What are you going to do? Hit me?"

She dropped her hands to her side and uncurled her fists. "Of course not."

"Good. Because I prefer to use my head"—he leaned forward—"to using either my heart or my fists." He stalked away before she could calm her anger enough to answer.

She searched frantically for the perfect retort as he widened the distance between them. "You stay away from my grandmother."

She slammed the heel of her hand into her forehead. That was really a clincher all right. Aaggh. Why could she never think of what she wanted to say when she was upset? No doubt she'd think of the perfect thing about two in the morning.

Not that it mattered. They were as far apart as the north from the south on how their grandparents should conduct their relationship. As they were on so many things. She grabbed the empty cups and headed inside to do something useful. She refused to allow herself even a hint of regret at the way things had gone south with the speed of a rocket ship.

Suddenly she laughed.

"What's so funny?" Annie asked. "Didn't I just see you and Steele practically ready to kill each other?"

"He thinks he should interfere with Nan and Henry's romance. I was just thinking what Nan would say to anyone poking his nose in her business. I hope Steele tries it, though I feel sorry for him if he does."

seven

Steele dropped to his chair, turned it away from the window, and stared at the bright geometric framed print on his wall. He felt as fractured as all those triangles and squares. He'd always liked the picture, even though it made no sense—no pattern, no reason for the arrangement.

His gaze fixed on a bright spot of purple. A tiny square in the midst of large orange, red, and green shapes. The same color as the flowers in the planter at J'ava Moi.

Why had she rearranged the planters so he didn't have to sit beside pink flowers? More important, why did he sniff the flowers and act all lovey-dovey? He grunted and felt an incredible disgust at himself. That was why he didn't believe in romance. It got a man all confused just when he needed to have his wits about him. And if it could happen to him, a lawyer, practiced in rational thought, a man who didn't believe in such foolishness in the first place, he could only imagine how the whole business of recreating scenes of first love could make it impossible for Pops to think straight.

As he'd said to Holly, the best thing would be for Pops and Jean to go back home and think about this whole business without the confusing trappings of picnics and flowers and late evenings. He chuckled. Eight o'clock didn't qualify as late in his books, but it seemed to in his grandfather's.

He rubbed his chest where Holly had planted her finger. He knew a flash of regret that she'd shifted from starry-eyed to combative so quickly. Which further proved how all those trappings could confuse a man. Sure, she was a beautiful woman, with her wavy brown hair and expressive brown eyes. He snorted. Looks were only skin deep, after all.

He pushed to his feet, strode over to stare at the purple square on the picture, then turned and without conscious thought crossed to the window to look down at the outdoor tables and flowers. He located the planter full of pink ones and shuddered. No way was he going to let himself get tangled up by such foolishness.

ॐ

Pops unlocked the door and walked into the apartment. Steele pointed at his boots, and the older man gave a long-suffering sigh, backed up, and grabbed his slippers. "Sissy footwear," he muttered and made a great show of tiptoeing into the living room in his slippers.

"Whatcha been doing? You and Jean."

"We've been out and about."

"Yeah. Doing what?"

Pops fixed him with a hard look. "You cross-examining me?"

Steele shrugged. "Just trying to show a little interest."

Pops headed for the fridge. "You ever fix a meal? There's nothing in here but junk food." He pulled out a leftover piece of pizza with two fingertips and dropped it into the garbage.

"There goes dinner," Steele said, laughing at the way Pops wrinkled his nose.

"I haven't eaten," Pops said. "And I don't want to go out."

"I'll order in. What do you like—Chinese or pizza?"

"A man could die of all this high-fat junk. I want a plain old meal—meat and potatoes and lots of veggies."

Steele joined Pops at the fridge, pulled open the freezer side, and dug out a package of sirloin steak. The plastic had cracked. The meat had streaks of freezer burn. "Here you go."

Pops drew back and refused to touch the meat. "That's disgusting. Grab your boots, boy. We're going shopping."

"I thought you were too tired to go out."

"Lesser of two evils." He looked at the steaks and shuddered. "I would have brought meat from home if I'd known this was the best you had to offer."

Steele shoved the steak back in the freezer and closed the door. "Something eating at you, Pops?"

"Just my hunger."

An hour later they returned with bags of groceries, enough to feed a small army, Steele figured. He hoped it didn't hint at Pops planning an extended stay. "You'll be headed back to the ranch soon, I suppose." He kept his attention on the potatoes he scrubbed.

"You telling me it's time to move on? 'Cause if you are, there're lots of motels in town."

Steele dried the potatoes, wrapped them in foil, and stuck them in the oven before he faced Pops. "You've been acting like a cow with a nail in her cud all evening. You want to tell me what's going on, or am I expected to shut up and ignore your snipes?"

Pops's expression grew stubborn, then he sighed and pulled himself up on a stool. "It's Jean."

Steele nodded. He'd seen this coming. The old guy was going to get hurt all over again.

"I want to marry her. I should never have walked away from her fifty years ago, though I don't regret a minute of my time with your grandmother. It's just that Jean and I have"—he waggled his hands—"something. A connection I can't explain. She makes me feel good about myself. She does thoughtful little things." He must have seen the skepticism in Steele's face. "Yeah, I know you'll mock, but she does romantic things. Your grandmother never did. I bought flowers and gifts. Your grandmother was far more practical, but it makes a person feel special to be the recipient, you know."

Steele didn't, but he wasn't going to say so. Nor was he going to acknowledge the hollow echo deep inside him as he remembered Holly saying something similar. "So what's the problem?"

"There are many things to consider—money, property. . . ." He sighed deeply. "So many choices and decisions. It gives me a headache just thinking of it. Maybe I'm too old for this sort of nonsense."

Maybe Pops had begun to discover things on his own. "Pops, why complicate your life? Why not go home and enjoy what you've worked so hard to build?"

"A man gets lonely."

Steele thought of all the lonely, unhappily married men he'd seen. "Pops, a man can be married and still be lonelier than he imagined."

"You are far too cynical for a young man. I'm not afraid I'd be lonely if I married Jean. I just don't care for all the decisions that need to be made."

"Maybe it's time to forget this business." He kept his voice soft, almost pleading. *Please, Pops, go home before you get hurt. Before you buy yourself a whole set of problems you don't want to deal with.*

"No. Avoiding problems is never a way to solve them. Jean and I have some decisions to make, and it's time to make them." He slapped his palm on the counter. The harsh noise caused Steele to jump. "I know what I'm going to do. Jean and I took a long drive once. Out toward Anaconda on the Pintler scenic route. We looped around to Deer Lodge and returned. Had a really good time as I recall. I'm going to take her on that trip, and we're going to deal with things."

Steele could imagine them confined to a small vehicle for hours with nothing to do but talk. "I'll tell you what. I'll drive. That way you and Jean can concentrate on the scenery."

Pops's eyes lit up. "Good idea. We can sit in the back, and I can hold her hand."

Steele resisted the urge to roll his eyes. Great. He thought he'd make it impossible for them to scheme in private; Pops saw it as an opportunity to cuddle in the back. Sometimes he couldn't believe they shared the same genes. Steele had obviously inherited more of his mother's genes than his father's.

As he plotted how to nip this little problem in the bud, he washed lettuce for a salad then went to the balcony and turned on the barbecue to grill steaks.

❧

Saturday morning dawned as bright and clear as only a Montana day could, promising never-ending sunshine.

Pops had shaved twice and slicked his hair down too many times for Steele to count. He headed for the door a half dozen times as Steele drank his second cup of coffee. Finally he jerked on his boots. "Come on, boy. What's holding you up? There's a lot to see and do before the day is out."

Steele gathered up his keys. "Pops, hold your horses."

But the older man hurried outside and stood by the SUV as Steele locked the apartment.

"I'll ride shotgun until we pick up the ladies."

Steele pulled himself behind the wheel before he answered. "You mean Jean." His gut warned him he couldn't be so fortunate.

"Holly's coming, too. No point in you being alone." Pops leered at him. "You pay attention, boy, and I'll show you how to win a woman's heart."

Steele's stomach did a strange little bounce—rising in a rocket launch arc at the idea of Holly at his side all day then plummeting with a mingling of dread and nervousness. He wanted nothing to distract him from being Pops's voice of reason throughout the day. Somehow he felt certain Holly's presence would prove exactly that—a distraction.

Steele gripped the steering wheel. Holly hadn't been part of the plan, but he could deal with it. He'd had worse surprises. Like the time he'd fallen off his horse and rolled to the bottom of a hill, scaring a porcupine. He'd found his feet faster than lightning and backed away from the angry little creature.

"Boy, stop your daydreaming and let's get moving."

His knuckles white, Steele drove away, heading downtown to historic East Pine Street.

Holly and Jean—holding a single purple daisy of some sort—waited on the sidewalk. Pops obviously wasn't the only eager one this morning.

Pops jumped out and opened the back door for Jean. She handed him the flower.

"What's this?"

"I remembered you asked the florist about gerbera daisies the other day. You said how bold they were. So I bought you one."

Pops took the flower, his gaze never leaving Jean's face. He brushed his knuckles against her cheek. "Thank you."

No mistaking the huskiness in Pops's voice. These little gestures made him feel special, he'd said. But as Steele watched the older man stand rooted to the sidewalk, he figured such nonsense only mucked up the old man's reasoning. It wasn't until Holly opened the passenger-side door that Pops and Jean seemed to remember they weren't the only two people in the world.

Holly climbed in beside Steele. "Good morning."

He nodded. "Morning."

She studied him. Her smile faded. "How nice of you to offer to take Nan and Henry on this trip."

Steele heard the warning in her voice, knew she suspected him of ulterior motives, and ignored her.

"Nan is excited. She hasn't been back in fifty years."

"I expect things will have changed." What he meant, what he wanted to say was, *Holly, get real. Only fools and romantics think you can recreate something fifty years after the fact.* Pops wasn't the same man, and Jean was certainly not the young, innocent woman of fifty years ago.

"So you've mentioned a time or two." She snapped open a map. "This should be fun."

He didn't miss the emphasis on "should" any more than he mistook her subtle warning.

They locked gazes and did silent battle for a moment. He sensed her drawing a mental line in the dust.

"Come on, boy," Pops boomed. "Time's a-getting away."

Steele tipped his chin in silent acceptance of her challenge. "Should be quite a day," he murmured, pulling away from the curb and heading out of town.

Jean settled back. "The country is just as pretty as I remember it. Rolling hills like draped fabric. Each fold growing more and more gray in the distance. Never have seen anything prettier."

Steele had to wonder where she'd spent the past half century. "Where's home for you?"

"Seattle. Tom and I bought a house there shortly after we married."

"Which," Holly murmured, "is now worth a fortune."

"Point taken." It didn't negate all the other obstacles to a relationship between the older pair.

"I remember we stopped often to look at the sprawling vistas," Jean said.

Steele kept up a steady speed. After all, as Pops had said numerous times already, they had a lot of miles to cover.

"Nan, we'll stop at the next pullout." Holly said her grandmother's name, but Steele knew she spoke to him.

"Oh, don't bother for me. I know Steele wants to get—"

"Exactly where are you going in such a hurry?" Pops demanded.

Steele lifted his hand off the wheel in a sign of defeat. "Who was chomping at the bit not more than forty-five minutes ago?"

"I wanted to start the trip, not hurry and end it. You gonna be like this, and I'll wish I'd brought my own vehicle. Jean wants to stop and admire the scenery. What's wrong with that?"

The air inside the SUV grew heavy with combined disapproval from the others. Steele gave a grin that felt too small for his mouth. "My misunderstanding. I thought we had a destination." He saw a turnout and pulled over. The others piled out of the vehicle and gathered at the edge of the road to admire the deep valley before them.

"It's beautiful," Jean said, turning to smile sweetly at Pops. Poor old Pops practically melted like hot butter right on the spot.

Steele stood beside the vehicle, arms crossed over his chest, a feeling of frustrated fury tightening his lungs.

Holly pulled herself away from the view and came to his side. "Steele, what's wrong?"

"Nothing." Except he didn't want Pops hurt.

"Glad to hear that. Would it kill you to show it?"

He relaxed his arms, leaned back on his heels, and forced a smile to his lips.

A few minutes later, they were on their way. The two in the back talked softly. Steele strained to hear what they said. Holly, consciously or not, ran interference. "I brought a map. It's got all sorts of information. Did you know the Number One highway is the oldest paved road in Montana?"

He grunted. Didn't know. And wondered why he should care.

They reached Philipsburg, according to Holly's running commentary, the liveliest ghost town in the West. "Twice the town has won the award for the prettiest painted place."

"My, it's changed since we were here," Jean said, peering out the side window. "It's very pretty, isn't it?"

"Look." Pops pointed past Jean's shoulder. "There's a little courtyard and some tables. We can get coffee there."

Steele pulled to the curb before anyone could suggest stopping.

"What a pretty spot," Jean said. "Holly, just think what you could do if you had that much outdoor space. Look at the pots of flowers and trees. And the artwork."

Holly pressed her nose to the side window. "It's lovely."

"Henry." Jean's voice was as round as the daisy on the seat between the two. "I do believe we stopped at this very spot. I don't remember the patio; but I recall a bench beneath the sign on that building, and I remember you telling me about the silver mines and the manganese needed in World War One." She clasped her hands together in front of her chest. "We had such a good time. We sat right there"—she pointed to the place—"for a long time and discussed so many things— our faith, our families, our dreams. We prayed together for God to lead us regarding our future." Her voice grew husky. "I believe this is a sign—remembering how we asked God to direct us. I've been praying to know how we should proceed." She sent a shy smile to Holly, including Steele. "Henry has asked me to marry him. I've hesitated because there are so many things to consider. It's not like being young and having nothing to think about but the future."

Steele had done his best to restrain his frustration at the flowers, the impractical dreams, the purposeful disregard for facts, but Jean's sudden revelation grabbed at his throat. Suddenly he could keep quiet no longer. "Enjoy coffee. Enjoy the town. Buy some little souvenir if you like. But don't let flowers and faded memories cloud your thinking. Jean's right. You both need to hesitate and get your feet back on the ground before you make any big decisions you could regret later."

Silence filled the vehicle. He knew they all stared at him, but he pulled the keys from the ignition and grabbed the door handle.

"Steele, you're out of line." Pops's voice growled his anger.

"Jean, you'll have to forgive him. He has no business speaking that way. Boy, you're far too much like your mother. Don't get me wrong. She's a good woman, but she sees no value in anything but work. I'm sure she'd stomp a flower if it crossed her path."

His gut burning, Steele wrenched the door open and strode away.

He didn't realize Holly had followed him until she grabbed his elbow. Still, he didn't slow his steps until she edged around him and blocked his way. "Steele, what gives you the right to speak to my grandmother like that? Or your grandfather, for that matter. What is wrong with you?"

He saw the brick walls of the building beside him. Saw a sign. Read the words without knowing what they said. "Nothing. I'm worried about my grandfather. I don't want to see him hurt."

"Aren't they entitled to make their own choices? They're not exactly senile."

"Don't you think they should take some time and think about what they're doing? A break. Go home." He said the words woodenly, not thinking them, not feeling them, simply repeating them from the arguments he'd provided himself for days.

"Steele, I get the feeling this isn't about Nan and Henry. It's about you. What are you running from?"

There were no flowers in sight. Just brick and board. Yet he had the same stupid, nameless, suffocating feeling he got when he saw pink flowers. He shuddered.

She maneuvered him toward a bench at the edge of the sidewalk and nudged him toward the wooden seat. He sat.

"Something's bothering you. What is it?" Like a soft spring

breeze, her voice pulled at his thoughts. But how could he tell her something he didn't understand? Pops's words echoed inside his head, tangling with his own confused thoughts. Work. Practical. *Stomp*—why did he shudder at the word? Flowers. Pink flowers. A thought tugged at the edges of his mind. A little boy kneeling, tears on his cheeks. Was he the boy? No way. He'd never been a crybaby.

"What's wrong?" Holly asked again.

"I don't know." He looked at her and resisted an urge to catch the strands of hair blowing across her cheek and tuck them back.

"Is it what Henry said about your mother?"

"No. Mom is very practical. She operates a Cat. Pushes dirt around."

Holly touched the back of his hand. "Tell me about your parents."

"Not much to say. They met when Mom asked for a job with the construction company. Threatened to sue Dad if he refused because she was a woman. He says she pestered him until he finally said okay. Said the same about getting married. She pestered him into it. Not that he doesn't adore her. I always think of them with Dad's arm around her waist standing at the side of a construction project discussing the work. They have a great relationship." He felt he had to make sure she knew that.

"So you think every relationship should be as practical?"

"Yes. No. I don't know." What was there about this woman that turned his brain to powder?

Her hand still rested on his, and he grew aware of its gentle weight. The boiling turmoil of a few minutes ago settled into a simmer, and he slowly relaxed.

"Seems to me all kinds of relationships work. It's not up to us to judge, so long as they do work," she said.

"Are you talking about Pops and Jean?"

"Partly. I don't think they need us to tell them how to run their lives. In fact, I hope I can learn something from them."

"Uh huh." A noise meant to be noncommittal. He jerked to his feet. "I'm going to poke around the shops." It beat thinking about the crying young boy and how it related to Pops and Jean. If indeed it did, which seemed highly unlikely. He stood and waited for Holly. "Want to come along?"

"I might want to buy flowers or something frilly."

"I might want to buy a different map."

She chuckled. "One with nothing but the miles and the names of the towns, I suppose."

"You must have read my mind." ·

She came to his side and nudged him with her shoulder, causing him to stumble. He grabbed her hand and pulled her to his side to stop her from repeating it. She swung their joined hands as they marched along the street. Holly browsed through gift shops and boutiques while Steele picked up a colorful brochure describing the historic buildings. He found the history fascinating. They passed Pops and Nan several times, and each time he felt a pang that he wasn't fulfilling his goal and keeping them from discussing marriage. He blinked. Had that been his goal? He thought he only wanted to make sure they didn't make foolish decisions. When had marriage become the foolish thing he worried about?

Holly must have felt his start of surprise. "What's up with you? You're acting so strange today."

"That's hardly flattering."

"You're the guy who likes his feet planted on terra firma.

I would think flattery would be an insult."

"Flattery is an insult because it's insincere." He grabbed her hand and pulled her from the store. "We'd better continue this journey." He'd better get himself sorted out before he lost his way.

They rounded up Pops and Jean and headed down the road. Everyone was quiet as they drove. Steele blamed himself and his out-of-line comments about their relationship. He couldn't ignore the tension.

"Pops, I'm sorry I spoke out of turn."

"Boy, I'm sorry if I insulted your mother."

"You didn't. Did you?"

"Didn't mean to."

"Okay then. Now tell me what you want to do next."

"Lunch," three voices chorused.

Determined to make up for his earlier behavior, Steele repeated the historical information about Philipsburg. They passed Georgetown Lake, and he scoured his mind to remember everything he could about the lake. "At one time special trains came to the lake from Butte with chairs on open gondola cars." He rattled on about the mountains, the mines, the forest service, and even remembered to mention the huge elk herds of the area. Anything to keep from thinking about the little boy with the tear-stained face, pink flowers, and Jean and Pops. They seemed to be connected, which made no sense whatsoever.

At one point he glanced in his mirror, saw Jean, her eyes closed, her head resting on Pops's shoulder. He'd put her to sleep. Given her a reason to nestle against Pops. Hardly his intention.

He instantly shut up.

They pulled in at Anaconda, where the main street seemed

to disappear into the foot of a mountain. Pops insisted they have a "real" meal, and they stopped at a steak joint.

"Great tour guide," Pops said as they waited for their meal. "Had no idea you knew so much about the area."

Steele nodded. "I read a lot."

"Talk a lot, too," Holly murmured, low so the other two didn't hear, then turned to include Jean and Pops. "Sure surprised me when he spouted all that information."

Jean chuckled. "I slept through most of it. Sorry."

Steele was thankful the steak arrived at that point, and he gave it his total attention. He didn't need anyone to point out how strange he'd been acting. From rude to talkative. He wished he knew what was wrong with him.

When Holly excused herself later to visit the ladies' room, he slipped away, saying he needed to check the oil in the SUV. He popped the hood and pulled out the dipstick. Of course it didn't need oil. He'd checked it last night. Had it changed a week ago. But he needed *his* dipstick checked. This whole day had gone from bad to worse, and it was only half over. He felt Holly's presence like something under his skin even before she spoke.

"Everything okay?"

No. He'd never felt less okay. She meant the SUV, of course. "Yup."

"I shouldn't have said that about you talking too much. I'm sorry. I realize you're doing your best to entertain Nan and Henry. It's very thoughtful of you."

He straightened, turned to stare at her. A compliment? Her approval slid along his senses like sweet perfume. This time he did tuck back those wandering lengths of hair. His fingers lingered on her smooth cheek. "You're beautiful." He couldn't believe he'd said the words aloud. "Sorry."

She caught his hand before he could jerk back. "Don't be sorry. I don't mind hearing compliments once in a while. Thank you."

Her eyes filled with something soft and inviting.

He curled his fingers around hers and felt her face beneath his knuckles. He studied her smiling lips and thought about kissing her.

Then the confusion of the day centered down on this woman. They fought like cats and dogs, and yet here he was longing to kiss her. He needed a checkup from the neck up.

She saw his sudden silent withdrawal and slipped away.

He turned to close the hood, wondering if he should slam his head between the pieces of metal. He couldn't remember ever feeling so torqued up inside.

"Next stop Deer Lodge," Pops said, holding the back door open for Jean.

"What's there?" Steele directed his question to Pops, but it was Holly he watched as she scooted to the passenger seat and snapped the map open. He'd offended her somehow. He just wasn't sure how or what to do about it.

"Auto museum, old Montana prison, cowboy collectibles, gun collection," Holly read from the map.

"We want to see the old autos," Pops said. "Even though we're probably older than lots of them."

"We'll have to be careful, or they'll want to keep us in the museum," Jean said, and the two of them chuckled like a couple of Laurel and Hardy movie nuts.

Holly sent them a wide smile, and Steele let himself relax. "I'd like to see the prison." Surely a visit to such a cold, cruel place would put him firmly back on his feet.

eight

Holly put on her sunglasses and adjusted her seatbelt. For a moment at the side of the vehicle, she'd thought Steele meant to kiss her. She tried to analyze her feelings.

Disappointment? A little, she admitted. She couldn't deny she felt drawn to him in ways defying reason. And not just today. Somehow, the more time they spent together, the more her feelings toward him shifted.

A touch of concern? That, too. All day she'd sensed a tension about him, as if he were fighting himself. It made her ache to hug him and tell him whatever bothered him could be fixed if not by talking then certainly by prayer. And she didn't mean the kind of chatter that had him talking nonstop for over an hour as if he feared silence. He'd gone out of his way to entertain them for the last part of the morning, which was cute and charming.

And wary? For sure. He was a man who confessed he despised the things she considered important. The man hated pink flowers. What was with that?

Yet she had hoped he'd kiss her. Felt certain he would. Then something happened to change his mind. She gave a deprecating smile. Probably the man remembered her penchant for romance, and it scared him.

Not that she intended to let it ruin her day. Nan and Henry were having a good time, and that made everything else less important.

They headed down the highway to more adventure. She expected the older couple to be tired, wanting to nap after the heavy lunch, but the food seemed to have energized them. Henry was a good storyteller and soon had them laughing at his tales of cow wrestling, bull stomping, and calf busting on the ranch. A time or two Holly wondered at the complete accuracy of his stories. They seemed a little too big to be real. She stole a glance at Steele. He met her look, grinned, and rolled his eyes.

She choked back laughter. And suddenly the road seemed smoother. All too soon they arrived at the museum site.

"You two antiques can look at the old cars," Steele said. "I'm going to visit the prison. Holly, you want to come with me?"

She was surprised and touched that he would arrange for Nan and Henry to wander off by themselves and quickly agreed to stay with Steele. She watched the older couple head into the auto museum, holding hands and nudging each other, laughing at secret jokes. "How nice of you to give them this time alone."

He grinned and looked pleased.

She patted his shoulder. "I'm beginning to think you're a romantic after all."

Instantly his face settled into hard lines.

There was something to be said for knowing when to keep her mouth shut. This would have been one of those times. One thing this man did not want to be called was romantic. But she wouldn't let one slip ruin the rest of the day and grabbed the brochure for a self-guided tour of the prison. "Lead on. Let's see where the bad guys were sent."

"This is my sort of museum." He snagged the brochure from her and took her hand.

She almost tripped at the doorway. Maybe she was wrong. Could be the man knew more about romance than he let on, because holding hands as he read from the brochure seemed to her to be pretty romantic.

"No running water or sewer when it was first built," he read. "Just two buckets. One for sewage and another for water. Sounds appealing."

"Not."

They laughed, their gazes locking for a heartbeat. She turned away first.

They read and joked and laughed around the perimeter of the prison. The sun shone down, and the reason for the buildings seemed far removed from them until they stepped into the cellblocks and Steele read stories of some of the inmates. By the time they got to the "hole"—a dark, cement room—Holly could no longer smile, and Steele had grown quiet. They backed out and stared around the prison yard.

"It's so bleak," Holly murmured.

"Utilitarian," Steele insisted. He grabbed her hand and bolted out the exit into the open air.

Holly laughed. "That's a tour I'll remember for a long time."

"I should never have suggested it."

"Why not?"

He caught a strand of hair between his fingers and examined it. "You belong in sunshine and flowers." His expression grew bleak, and he sank to the nearby bench and buried his face in his hands.

"It's only an old jail. We can be thankful times have changed."

"It's not the jail." His voice was muffled.

"Then what?"

"I don't know." He sounded angry.

She sat beside him and put her hand lightly on his shoulders. She wished she could do more, but the man had to find his own way to whatever truth he needed. She prayed God would help him and felt compelled to let Steele know her concern. "Dear God, help Steele deal with whatever is bothering him."

"I keep seeing this little boy in my mind."

"Who is the little boy?"

"I think it might be me."

"Why does it bother you to see him?"

He jerked his head up and stared away. "Because he's crying. He shouldn't be crying."

She felt the harshness of his pain like scraping her fingertips over the rough cement in the prison behind them.

"He's just a little boy, isn't he? Don't little boys cry?"

"Not over dumb things." He jerked to his feet and strode away, swung around, and returned. He stood in front of her, his fists clenched.

She raised her gaze to his face, saw desperation quickly replaced with fury. Slowly she rose. "What were you crying about?"

"Nothing." He snapped around to stare at the museum door. "I don't remember."

Holly went to his side, touched his arm. "I'm sure the little boy didn't think it was dumb. Aren't the child's opinions valid?"

She felt him stiffen, felt a sort of expectant surprise, as if he held his breath. She knew her words hit a nerve and prayed he would face whatever it was he kept denying. Her heart squeezed as she thought of the crying child that was Steele. It pained her to think of him hurting. Suddenly she realized whatever had caused him to cry back then still bothered him today. *Oh, God, pour Your healing into his heart. Comfort that little boy who is now this man.* She wished she could see his expression, but the sunshine off the windows they faced allowed her only a flash.

She pressed the side of her finger against her upper lip to stop the stinging in her nose. She wanted to comfort him, show him love. She slipped her arm around his waist and hugged gently, fearing he would resist her touch, but he allowed her to hold him.

A sigh whooshed from his depths. He relaxed inch by inch as she held him. "Sometimes," she whispered, "hurting boys just need a hug."

He dropped his arm across her shoulders. "Thank you."

The air seemed awash with silvery light, which settled around her heart and lungs like a fine necklace draped around her neck. She pressed her cheek against his arm. He wore a short-sleeved, button-front shirt in soft cotton. She'd noticed how the pale tan color made his eyes glow with amber highlights. Now she noted the warmth of the material caressing her cheek like a sun-laden day at the lake. A shadow fell across the window, and she saw their reflection and gasped. Here they were hugging each other in full view of God and everyone—it was the *everyone* she worried about. What would people think? The warmth in her cheeks intensified, and she put several inches between them even as Steele jerked his arm from across her shoulders and backed away.

Nan and Henry stepped out of the museum.

One look at her grandmother's grin and twinkling eyes and Holly knew Nan had been one of the spectators.

"Good to see you learning from my example," Henry boomed as he draped his arm across Nan's shoulders. He pulled her close and whispered in a voice that could be heard for a block, "Might be hope for these two after all."

Holly didn't dare glance at Steele. She feared his expression would be thunderous.

"You ready to head home?" Steele asked, his voice revealing nothing. He grabbed Holly's hand and headed for the vehicle.

She stole a look then. It might be wishful thinking, but he looked pretty pleased with life. She laughed soft and low in the back of her throat. This feeling of unity with him might be short lived, but she wasn't about to waste it by wondering when he'd shift back into his practical, no-nonsense, lawyer mode.

He opened the door and held her elbow as he guided her to the front seat. She gave him a smile no doubt as full of happiness as her heart, which had developed this strange, alarming ability to do a Snoopy dance.

"Thank you," she said as she settled on the soft leather seat of the SUV. She met his gaze, overflowing with something so tender and fragile she feared taking a breath would shatter it.

"Hey, you two," Henry growled. "I thought we were going home."

Steele glanced at his grandfather, effectively releasing Holly from the uncertain tension.

As they headed back down the highway toward Missoula, Holly tried to sort out what had just happened and how she felt about it. She tried to be rational and failed. She could think of nothing but gratitude. Something had taken place in Steele's heart, some sort of healing, and in that moment he'd reached for her and smiled his favor. She wanted to hug herself with the joy of it.

The bubbling feeling of it couldn't be contained. She had to find an outlet. A victory dance couldn't be performed in the confines of the vehicle. A *rah-rah* cheer would scare the others. Silly grinning out the side window wasn't entirely satisfying. Talk was the only release available at this moment.

She shifted so she could see into the backseat. "Henry, did Nan tell you about the banquet Steele and I are planning? It's next week." She didn't wait for his answer but rushed on with details of the orphans, the bands, and the decorations. Both grandparents laughed as she described the argument about what form the decorations should take.

"I'm actually eager to see how the red, white, and blue theme will play out."

Steele laughed. "Still doubtful?"

"Not a bit."

He pulled his gaze briefly from the road, his glance rife with meaning.

She knew neither of them meant the decorations alone.

"Do we have volunteers to help set up?" he asked, his attention back on his driving.

"So far it's just you and me."

Another quick glance. Another silent message. He grinned with unusual warmth, as if the idea of the two of them pleased him. Of course, it might be wishful thinking on her part.

"I'll do some recruiting Sunday." His tone informed her

people would be agreeing to help.

"Are there still tickets available? Jean, why don't we go? Sounds like fun and a cause I'd like to support."

Holly couldn't think of anyone she'd sooner have there than Nan and Henry. And about a hundred others.

❧

"It looks great," Holly said. The red, white, and blue bunting hung from a stage created to look like a bandstand. Streamers hung from the ceiling. The patriotic theme carried through to the napkins on the table and the floral centerpieces.

"I didn't realize it would be so much work."

"Good thing you got so many people to 'volunteer.'" A dozen people, mostly young men, had appeared to set out tables and chairs and help put up streamers. They'd done their part and left. Only Steele and Holly remained to take care of last-minute details.

"I can hardly wait," Holly said. "I sent Heather an e-mail reminding her tomorrow is the big day. Do you have an estimate of the income yet?"

"We still have a few bills to pay, so I won't know for sure until tomorrow." He touched Holly's chin. "Don't look so worried. It looks like the orphanage will be able to repair the entire roof. Why don't we put out a donation box in case people want to donate more?"

His touch crowded her mind, made her think of a flower-filled arbor, long walks in the moonlight, staring up into the stars and dreaming mutual dreams. She pulled her thoughts back to center. "Wouldn't it be wonderful if we raised enough for the orphanage to expand? Heather is always telling me how crowded they are. She says they need more space but never have enough funds."

He trailed his finger along her cheek, filling her with such longing she feared it showed in her eyes.

"You are the most generous person I know," he said. "I can't think of anyone else who would pour themselves into an event the way you have to help children you've never even met."

His undeserved words pleased her. "You've worked as hard as I have."

He chuckled, bringing her curious gaze up to his eyes. He looked at her with dark intensity, searching deep into her soul. Her smile faded as, equally intent, she sought beyond his eyes into what this moment meant.

"I didn't start out caring about orphans. It was only a job assigned to me."

Her smile returned at his confession. Since their public hug outside the old prison, she'd been aware of a change in him, a softening, a gentleness she had only rare glimpses of in the past.

Somewhere in the distance a phone chirped. Hers.

Neither of them moved. He trailed his finger back along her cheek and across her chin, pausing there. She caught her breath, waited as he studied her mouth.

The chirping stopped.

He lowered his head and—

The phone rang again.

He pulled back. "Someone wants you."

She nodded, choking back disappointment. She located the phone near the door, tucked into her bag, and flicked it on without checking the caller ID.

"Hello." Her voice sounded as tense as she felt.

"Hi, honey, did I interrupt you?"

"No, Dad. I was at the far end of the banquet hall. How are you?"

Her father didn't answer. "Dad?" Nothing. She pulled the phone away to make sure it hadn't shut down. Nope. All systems bright and cheerful. She pressed the phone back to her ear. "Dad, are you there?"

"Holly, I have some bad news."

Her knees seemed to disappear. She grabbed at the wall, eased herself down to the bench. "Mom?" she whispered.

"She's gone."

"Gone? What happened?" She imagined an accident on the mountain roads. She always warned Mom she drove too fast.

"She didn't say. Just packed her bag and said it was over."

"She's not dead?"

"Feels like she is. She left me, Holly. She left me."

Holly sucked in air. Mom was alive. That was good news. She'd left Dad. That was bad news. Holly stared at the pine board floor as she tried to take it in. "Mom can't have left you. You guys have a good marriage."

"I thought so, but I guess she didn't."

Holly tried to make sense of her dad's announcement. "Maybe she's just upset at something. Go talk to her."

"I don't know where she is. I haven't heard from her since she left. It's been a week. Has she called you?"

"Not in days."

"You'll let me know if you find out where she is?"

"Of course."

Her father said good-bye and broke the connection.

Holly leaned over her knees and moaned.

Steele found her like that, sat beside her, and put his arm

around her. "Holly, what's wrong?" He rubbed her shoulder.

She turned into his arms and buried her face against his chest. Shudders racked her body. She did not cry. She felt nothing but shock.

"Who was on the phone?" Steele probed gently.

"My dad. Mom's left him."

Steele rubbed her back, stroked her hair. "I'm sorry. Perhaps it's temporary."

She pretended she didn't hear the doubt, the resignation in his voice. She understood he'd seen too many marriages go down the tubes to be convinced of his words, but she didn't want to deal with the reality of his viewpoint. Right now she just wanted the comfort of his arms.

"I've always believed in forever marriages because of them. They've had problems and dealt with them. They share the same joys and hopes and dreams. How could this happen?"

She was thankful he didn't spout meaningless platitudes.

"How will I tell Nan?"

"I don't know. Must you?"

"If she finds out I knew and didn't tell her, she'll never forgive me." He smelled good, felt warm and strong. "I don't know what to do," she wailed.

"Would you like me to pray?"

"Oh, please." She pushed herself off his chest. It hardly seemed appropriate to be thinking of the way he smelled and felt while talking to God.

He took her hand and bowed his head. "Heavenly Father, this is not good news. We ask You to work things out according to Your will."

He made it sound as if things could end in more than one way. She didn't like that idea. But he'd asked for God's will. God created marriage to last a lifetime. His will would surely be for Mom and Dad to get back together.

"Thank you," she whispered. "I have to believe this is only a bump in the road."

He cupped her cheek and turned her to face him. "Keep believing. Keep trusting. It's what you do best. It's one of the things I like about you."

And before she could do more than blink at his admission he liked something, anything, about her, before she could think to ask what other things he liked, he lowered his head and kissed her. She sighed and forgot everything she should wonder about. Forgot everything but how right this felt.

He lifted his head and smiled at her as he searched her eyes. Whatever he saw there, his smile widened, and he kissed her again then reluctantly, it seemed to her, pulled her gently to her feet and led her toward the door. "It's time to go home."

She made a protesting noise, and he chuckled, the sound strangely hypnotic.

"We've never really discussed this, but"—he paused—"do you have an escort to the banquet?"

Never really discussed it? More like never mentioned it. She knew she wouldn't have time to be a proper date, so she'd planned to go alone. "No," she said. "No one."

"Then may I be your official escort?"

She laughed, a sound of pure joy that found its way from some unfamiliar place behind her heart. The idea of being Steele's date made her momentarily forget her dad's announcement. "I'd like that."

He dropped her off at her apartment. As she climbed the

steps, she tried to cling to the feeling of security when he'd held her, the oneness expressed by his kiss. But by the time she turned her key in the lock, the pleasure and wonder of it had been consumed by worry about her parents. Nan had already gone to bed. Holly tiptoed into the living room and dialed Mom's cell phone, receiving a message the customer was out of area. *Mom, where are you? What's going on?* She left a message begging her mother to call.

â

When the phone jangled the next morning, she dove for it. Recognizing her mother's hello, Holly sank to the couch in relief. "Mom, where are you?" She repeated her silent words of the night before. "Dad phoned me. What's going on?"

"I had to leave." In faltering tones, her mother told her story. "A man stayed at the resort. A good-looking man with a quick smile. He paid me compliments. Made me feel special. You know how romantic I am. How I like those little gestures."

"Guess I inherited that from you."

"Well, I'm going to tell you, there's nothing romantic about being unfaithful."

Holly's stomach clenched. The air blasted out of her as if someone had stomped on her chest. "Mom, you didn't—" She couldn't think it, let alone say it. "Say you didn't."

"It never went that far."

"Thank God. Where are you?" Mom gave the name of a friend.

"Dad's really worried. He wants to call you."

"I can't talk to him."

"Why not? You two have always talked about everything."

"What I did was wrong. Besides, this is only a symptom

of a faltering marriage. I just feel like there's no magic left."

"Walking away from Dad is wrong. Didn't you always tell me two wrongs don't make a right? Mom, at least talk to him."

"I will on one condition—you promise not to tell him what I told you about. . .well, you know what."

"I'll leave that up to you."

They said tearful good-byes. As soon as the connection ended, Holly dialed her father's number and told him to call her mother.

"Did she say what was wrong?"

"You need to ask her. Dad, send her flowers. Make her feel special. That's all she needs."

"I have to go. I have to call your mother."

Holly said good-bye. She leaned back into the cushions and groaned.

Nan sat at the table listening to every word. "What's going on?"

"Mom left Dad. She doesn't seem happy in their marriage anymore. She said the magic was gone."

Nan tsked. "Your mother always did think with her heart rather than her head."

Holly knew she was like her mother in that way. She liked romance, feeling special. She liked the charm and enchantment of flowers and cards, the concrete evidence of love. "Isn't that an okay thing?"

"Child, the head should always rule the heart."

"I don't understand."

"Feelings are great. God created us with emotions. But feelings should always be guided by facts. Sometimes I don't feel like God loves me. Does that change His love? No. So instead of believing my weak emotions, I trust His love. A man and woman marry, usually with hearts overflowing with emotional love. Do you suppose that impassioned feeling lasts day after day?" She chuckled, though Holly failed to see anything amusing. "Believe me, it would be exhausting if it did. But while the feelings wax and wane, the commitment is consistent. Feelings are subject to facts."

Holly considered Nan's words as she made coffee and toasted bagels for breakfast. "But, Nan, doesn't love need to be fed to survive?"

She felt Nan's quiet study of her before her grandmother added, "Love is many things. People need different aspects of it at different times in their lives."

Holly left a short time later, Nan's words replaying in her mind. She couldn't imagine what Mom needed at this time of her life except for Dad to show his love in romantic ways. She was grateful she was too busy most of the day to fret about it and had to hurry home early to prepare for the banquet, leaving Meggie to end the day on her own.

nine

Steele looked at the corsage in his hand—a white orchid to be worn around the wrist. Pops's idea. Just as it was his grandfather's idea for them to travel separately tonight. He insisted he'd pick up Jean, and then Steele could come for Holly. Steele snorted. Good thing Pops was too old for Holly. They would have been soul mates—both so romantic.

He climbed the steps and knocked at the door. Holly pulled it open. He felt his chin dangling. With great effort, he clanged his mouth shut.

Her dress skimmed over her like spun silver. She'd pulled her hair into a bouncing creation on top of her head. Tiny curls cascaded from it down her neck and in front of her ears. He reached out and tugged one curl and laughed as it sprang back into place. She'd done something with her eyes so they looked bigger, darker, more full of love and trust, though he wondered if he didn't detect a hint of worry. No doubt concern about her parents' marital problems.

"You're beautiful." One word for the way she looked? He needed the whole dictionary, and even that would be inadequate.

"You're looking mighty fine yourself." She touched his tie, straightening it. Her fingers brushed his chin, practically stalling his heart.

"For me?" She nodded toward the corsage box.

"Hope it's all right."

She opened it and slipped the flower over her wrist. "Perfect. Thank you." She placed a quick kiss on his chin. A butterfly kiss that echoed inside his stomach and multiplied a thousand times. If one small flower could fill her eyes with pleasure and make her react this way, he just might reconsider his feelings about flowers and romance.

He crooked his elbow and let a surge of pleasure fill his chest as she placed her hand on his arm. He led her down the stairs and into his vehicle.

She sighed as he climbed behind the steering wheel.

He didn't like the sound. Had he forgotten something? "What's wrong?"

"I don't feel much like partying. Not with Mom and Dad split up." She turned to face him, her expression worried. "Mom called." She shook her head. "I don't know what's going on with her. I wish I could tell you about it, but it's Mom's story."

He paused, grateful his fingers were on the keys in the ignition because he felt an incredible urge to pull her into his arms and comfort her as she had comforted him at the museum. Her touch and her words had eased the tension accompanying the memory of that crying little boy. He found he could let it go.

Slowly, trying to plan what to say and do, he reached for her hand and held it. "Holly, if there's anything I can do. . . ?"

She turned her hand, twined her fingers through his. "Thank you for offering. Let's go have a good time."

He promised himself he would do everything he could to ensure she enjoyed the evening. She deserved a reward for all her hard work and dedication.

The minute they stepped into the hall, several people

rushed up to them demanding Holly's attention.

"The coffeepot isn't working." "One of the judges called in sick." "Did you want—?"

Steele steered her through the questions. "Give her a chance to get in the door." He guided her to the head table. "I'll send someone to replace the judge," he murmured. "You explain the score sheets. I'll deal with the rest." He put the coffeepot on another outlet so it didn't blow the breaker. He made several flyby decisions then returned to Holly's side.

She brushed his hand. "Thank you, Steele. That was sweet."

Her touch filled his veins with warmth. He leaned over, intending to tell her again how beautiful she was, but Pastor Don showed up at Holly's side. He'd agreed to emcee the event and flipped through his notes. "It's time to start."

As he moved to the mike, Holly grabbed Steele's hand.

"It's going to be great," he said and led her to their places at the table. He could hardly wait until she discovered his surprise contribution.

Pastor Don welcomed everyone. "To get us all focusing on the real purpose of the evening, I ask you to sit back and enjoy a brief presentation."

The lights dimmed, and the slide show Holly and her friend had prepared began. COME AND JOIN THE BAND OF LOVE scrolled across the screen then pictures that faded and blended—crying babies, wide-eyed toddlers. For a minute Steele wondered if they were going to be inundated with pictures so sad that none of them would be able to eat. And then the music changed slightly, growing more upbeat. LOVE IS—and pictures of people touching others, handing out food and water, washing feet; staff hugging and comforting children, playing games with them, teaching them to read. The music gained another beat. Children sang in rollicking African melodies. A children's choir appeared on the screen, and then the pictures focused on boys and girls playing various rhythm instruments. The words SHARE YOUR LOVE—JOIN THE BAND scrolled across the screen. The pictures faded, and from the murky background came a picture of a beautiful African girl, about ten, he'd guess, her nose buried in a white flower, her eyes reaching out to the audience.

The screen faded to black.

Steele welcomed the moment before the lights came up again, giving him a chance to blink back the sudden sting in his eyes.

He felt the emotional silence around him and then an outburst of applause and cheers. "That was a great presentation. You and Heather did that?"

"I'm afraid neither of us can take credit. Her parents were over visiting, and when her father heard what we wanted, he took on the project. He's a hobby photographer. He did a great job, didn't he?"

"Excellent." He suspected some of the images would haunt him for a long time.

Pastor Don rose and prayed, asking for a blessing on the food and for the needs of the children to be met.

The food was excellent. Even the salads, Holly pointed out, matched the red, white, and blue theme. As the caterers cleaned up the main course and prepared to serve dessert, tea, and coffee, Steele got up to explain the band competition.

The bands, despite their funny names, were excellent.

Finally Freddie and the Bent Fenders won with their crowd-pleasing combination of blue grass and classic rock, combined with a touch of standup comic.

Holly grinned at him. "That was fun."

Steele nodded. "The music was great, too."

She blinked, glancing at their clasped hands, and color rose in her cheeks. He held on when she tried to pull away.

"I enjoyed the evening," she whispered. "Much more than I thought I would."

He hoped he'd been part of the reason. He had gone out of his way to make her laugh. Enjoyed teasing the little curls hanging down her neck.

Pastor Don took the mike again. "I think we all agree it's been a great evening." Cheers and applause. "Let's hope we've contributed to putting a new roof on the orphanage." More applause. "And we've had fun." Cheers and whistles. Freddie's drummer accompanied with a clash of cymbals. "Two people have put in an incredible amount of work to see that this evening was a success. Holly Hope and Steele Davis, come on up here." There was a loud drum roll.

Steele felt Holly twitch under his fingers. He pulled her to her feet and smiled encouragement as she glanced at him. Amid clapping and cheering, they walked to the front to stand by Pastor Don.

Pastor Don waited for the noise to die down.

"It began with the vision of one person." Someone handed him a bouquet of red roses, and he placed it in Holly's arms. "Holly, thank you for all your hard work. Thank you for caring about the work in Africa and for sharing your concern. I think all of us will now share a bit of your vision."

Steele's heart swelled with a mixture of pride and wonder

and amazement as Holly beamed at the audience. She leaned over to speak into the mike. "Thank you all for coming. Thank you for your generosity, but it was Steele who made sure you had chicken and not tofu, who decided the program would be more than a talent show. And wasn't it great?" More cheers and clapping and a drum roll. "Steele deserves the credit for taking care of all sorts of practical things I wouldn't have thought of. The sound system, the stage, even the coffee."

They might have been the only two people in the room at that moment as she smiled and nodded at him, her eyes dark, brimming over with emotion.

She'd just admitted she admired his practical side—the part she'd dismissed only a few weeks ago as unromantic—and by the way her eyes shone with gratitude and acknowledgment, he had to wonder if she realized love was so much more than flowers. He glanced at the orchid on her wrist. He'd noticed how often she admired it during the evening, each time smiling at him in a way that seemed full of promise, and he had to admit flowers served a purpose, too.

She pulled a red rose from the bouquet and tucked it into his lapel. "Thank you, Steele. You've been marvelous." The way she smiled at him made him dream she meant more than his practical help.

He thanked Holly and the audience. "I expect you were all moved by the plight of these children and by the heroic measures of the people trying to care for them. When Holly and I began to plan this banquet, I'd heard about the many thousands of children being left without adults in their lives. I'm sure you had, too. But Holly made me see it as more than statistics, more than a sad newspaper story. She's been praying this banquet would raise enough money for the roof, but there are so many needs. She made me care so much that I canvassed the downtown businesses, and I'm pleased to present her with"—he reached into his inside pocket and pulled out the check—"a check for five thousand dollars, thanks to the generosity of the good people of Missoula."

Tears filled Holly's eyes. She swallowed hard. And in front of Pastor Don and the whole audience, she kissed his cheek. "Thank you," she whispered then turned to the audience. Still whispering, not realizing they couldn't hear her, she said, "Thank you all."

Steele pulled her to his side. "She says thanks."

More laughter and clapping followed.

People began to leave. Pops and Jean found them and congratulated them on a good job before the older pair left. The caterers cleaned up. And then they were the only ones there.

He pulled her into his arms. "Holly, you did it. You raised enough money for the roof and more. You must be happy."

She touched his cheek. "We did it, Steele. I can't believe you did that on your own." Her brown gaze locked with his, filled with gentleness and something else. She searched his eyes, into the depths of his heart. He waited for her to see him as he was, to remember his practical nature, so different from her own, and pull back. Instead she let her gaze roam over his face like the touch of morning sun. He needed no more invitation and bent to meet her lips, as sweet and accepting as the woman herself.

His phone buzzed.

She withdrew.

He pulled her back, ignoring the sound, but whoever it was didn't hang up. The sound went on and on.

He grabbed the phone from his pocket, checked the display. Mike. "I'd better get this."

She nodded and turned away.

He wanted to reach for her, pull her back, explain it was only a pause. Instead he took the call. "Hey, Mike. What's up?"

"Man, where are you? It doesn't matter. I can't take any more."

Steele tensed at the desperate sound in Mike's voice. "What are you talking about?"

"Today is my wedding anniversary."

Steele pressed the heel of his hand to his forehead. He'd forgotten. He'd been so busy letting Holly and her romantic notions affect his thinking that he'd forgotten his own brother. This romance stuff was a land mine to a man's reason.

&

Holly moved away, keeping her back to Steele so he wouldn't see her frustration and disappointment. *Don't be silly, Holly.* The evening had exceeded expectations. Only this wasn't about the evening. This was about Steele and her. He'd kissed her. And she'd welcomed it. Enjoyed it even. Something had shifted between them. She couldn't say when it had occurred or what it meant—only that it felt both fragile and strong at the same time.

She wandered past the bare tables. The banquet had gone well. Steele had been attentive and charming. She touched the orchid on her wrist. Flowers even. The man was changing. Did he realize it? She'd hoped they'd have some private time to enjoy the aftereffects of the banquet, the glow of success, and talk about what was happening between them. Would it end now that they had no compelling reason to be together? She hoped not. She had grown to be genuinely fond of him. She huffed. Fond? What kind of word was that? Not the sort to describe the fledgling, demanding emotions within her chest.

She realized Steele had ended his conversation and was heading toward her. She trailed her finger across a nametag left behind on the table as she waited and wondered if he would pick up where they'd left off.

"Sorry about that. It was Mike. My brother."

She nodded, still not able to face him.

"I forgot today would have been his anniversary."

She heard something in his voice. Something she'd never heard before except for hints when she mentioned siblings. She turned and saw the harsh lines around his eyes. "I take it Mike was married."

"For a few years. And now divorced. That woman practically destroyed him. She might succeed yet." As he talked, he gathered her things and handed them to her. "He's talking real stupid. I have to find him and calm him down."

She'd never heard so much emotion in his voice nor seen so much pain in his eyes. "I'm going with you." She knew he'd argue. Knew he didn't want anyone to see him vulnerable. "I'll keep you company on the drive."

He hesitated then headed for the door. "I don't expect I'll have time to entertain you."

She ignored his blunt words, knew he was worried about his brother, felt grateful he hadn't dismissed her, hadn't insisted on taking her home.

They headed out of town and were soon on the highway. "I let music and flowers make me forget what really matters.

If something happens to Mike—"

They arrived at a construction site, piles of dirt pushed up into hills. They bounced along a rugged trail. Steele seemed to know where he was going. They arrived at some trailers. Steele shone his headlights at one, jumped out, and raced to the door. He wrenched it open and hit the inside lights. "Mike!" he roared. He disappeared inside, returned in a few minutes, and bolted back to the SUV. "He's been living on the site, but he isn't in there."

He was about to jerk the vehicle into gear when he stopped. "Do you hear that?"

Holly heard nothing but the SUV's engine.

Steele cut the motor and stepped out. "He's over there." He jumped back under the wheel, restarted the motor, and spun away with no regard for the rough ground.

The sound he'd heard soon grew audible to Holly. A deep-throated roar of a big machine. Steele pulled to a halt beside a huge yellow Cat. "Stay here," he murmured.

Like she had a choice. No way would she go out and wander around in this dark moonscape. But before she could answer, he was gone.

She hunkered down to wait. Sometime later, the roar of the big motor ended. She waited, but still Steele did not return. She leaned her head back and closed her eyes.

ᏽ

"Holly, wake up."

For a moment she thought she must be dreaming. Why else would she hear Steele's voice calling her from sleep? Then she felt the seat belt digging into her neck, the tingle in her legs from being crammed against the door, Steele's hand heavy on her shoulder as he shook her awake.

She sat there a moment, hesitant to drag herself back to reality.

"Holly?"

She could feel his breath on her cheek. "I'm awake." His hands were firm on her shoulders, a patch of warmth against her chilled body. She shivered. "I'm cold."

He pulled off his tuxedo jacket and wrapped it around her.

Still half asleep, she sighed. "Warm. Smells like you. Good."

He chuckled. "Holly, are you really awake?"

She yawned. "Getting there." She yawned again. "Is Mike okay?"

"Yeah, I guess so, but I don't think he should be alone right now. Can you drive the SUV and follow us?"

"Anywhere you want." Oh, my. She sounded like she meant the words as part of wedding vows or something.

"Just to my parents' house." His voice rang with amusement, which filled her with a sensation of enjoyment.

"Are you sure you're awake?" he asked. "Maybe you'd better get out and walk around for a minute."

She stepped outside, the cool air jolting her brain closer to alert. But she didn't intend to take one more step than required on the rough ground and, clutching the SUV, edged around to the driver's side.

Steele held the door open, touched the back of her neck as she climbed in, then leaned in to speak to her. "I really appreciate this."

She nodded and started the motor. He strode over to a half-ton truck. As he drove away, she followed, gritting her teeth against the bouncing of the vehicle on the rough ground.

They reached a gravel road, much less rough, and she

settled back. Realizing the jacket still hung around her shoulders, Holly breathed in his masculine scent. She wondered if he used an aftershave, or was the hint of ocean breezes and pine trees uniquely his?

He pulled to a halt in front of a house with wide cement steps. She stopped behind him. He hurried around to open the passenger door and wave his brother out. She got her first glimpse of Mike. He was as tall as Steele and as muscular. In the headlights, she saw he had the same angular facial structure. Lights came on inside the house, then the yard flooded with light. The door jerked open, and a man and woman hurried out. Steele's parents. His father looked like a younger version of Henry, and his mother—she tried to guess what the woman would look like not pulled suddenly from her sleep. She wore pajamas. Seemed rather squarish built, her hair as short as her husband's. In the harsh lights, she seemed almost masculine. Holly wondered if it was a true evaluation or her own prejudice at the way Steele described his mother as practical and businesslike.

Steele spoke briefly to them before they went to Mike and on either side of him led him toward the house. Steele hurried back to the SUV.

She climbed out to switch sides so he could take the wheel. "Do you want to stay? Because if you do, I could sleep in this or go back to Missoula and return for you in the morning."

"He'll be all right now. But thank you for the offer." He touched her cheek. "You've been very patient. Thank you."

His fingers lingered, making it hard for her to think. "What are friends for?"

"Friends? I guess that's progress from being pretty much

on the opposite side of things." He stepped aside so she could hurry around to the other door.

She welcomed the cool air on her face and hoped it would clear her brain. Friends? Was that what she wanted? She shook her head, sucked in a deep breath at the longing that filled her. She had to be suffering from sleep deprivation. *Please, God, help me be sensible.* She smirked at her choice of words. She, the confirmed romantic, praying for sense—*my, how things have changed.*

She climbed in beside Steele, and they headed back to the city.

"Mike and I had a long talk." Steele spoke slowly, as if sorting out his thoughts. "He's a little turned off by love and marriage and all that kind of stuff. I guess we were all raised to think it was foolish. Mom has no use for anything like flowers and what she calls romantic nonsense. You remember the little boy I told you about?"

"The one that is you?"

"Yeah. Me. I remember why I was crying."

She sensed he'd remembered something profoundly significant, and hardly dared breathe. She wanted to say something supportive but feared to drive him back into denial. Instead she prayed for wisdom to know when to speak and when to listen and for Steele—healing for this distant pain.

"It's all about pink flowers, which probably doesn't surprise you."

Actually it did, but all she said was, "Tell me about the pink flowers."

They came to the first traffic light. He turned right into an empty parking lot and pulled to a stop. He reached out and took her hand.

"Mom and Dad often took us along to their work sites. We played while they worked. I remember how I liked this new place. We weren't allowed to go into a few old buildings, but we had lots of other places to explore. We spent hours of fun there. I found an old garden. I remember the grass had grown into the plants. I had to push aside the tall blades to see the flowers that seemed to me to be hiding as if they had a secret. There was a whole row of pink flowers. I have no idea what they were. I just knew they were beautiful and, I thought, special. I decided to pick them. I thought I'd give them to Mom and she'd like them. But she rode her Cat toward me, waved me away, and plowed them all down. I tried to stop her. When she saw me waving, she stopped long enough to tell me to stay back. I sat at the edge of the field and cried."

He stared straight ahead. His voice grew hoarse. His hand tightened.

She welcomed the way it made her fingers press together. It hurt ever so slightly. Made her feel she shared his pain. And she continued to pray that God would lead him through this. She knew the memory carried far more pain than he would likely admit. She guessed he'd never shared this before. Perhaps never allowed himself to remember it. She felt as privileged as if he had picked all those pink flowers and brought them to her. She didn't dare move for fear of making him pull back into himself, and yet her arms ached to comfort the little boy Steele had been. But would the child—clothed in the body of a man taught to be manly— know how to accept such a gesture?

A car passed on the street, the sound muted and lonely. The headlights sliced across the tree at the edge of the parking lot. The leaves, gray and colorless in the night, fluttered like birds in a courting dance, seeking to gain attention and approval from their desired one. She pressed her lips together. *Oh, Steele, if only I could kiss away your hurt and make it all better.*

Where had his mother been when he needed hugging? Why had she denied her child this basic motherly duty? Wouldn't most mothers consider it a privilege? For a moment she allowed herself the luxury of anger at Steele's mother. Then she pictured the way the woman had taken Mike's arm and led him into the house. She knew she cared and showed it in her own way.

"When she found me crying, she said flowers didn't matter. And men didn't cry. I don't know how many times we were told men don't cry. Tonight Mike cried. And I realized Mom was wrong. Men can cry."

She sensed he struggled with something momentous and squeezed his hand, hoping he felt her support.

"I remember telling Mom that Grandpops liked flowers. He was always buying them for Grandma. She said Pops acted foolish sometimes. Said no man should make a fool of himself over a woman."

He paused. His fingers twitched against her palm.

"That's why I don't want Pops marrying Jean. I'm afraid he's making a fool of himself over a woman."

Suddenly so many things were clear to Holly. "Steele, I think you and Mike made a very important discovery tonight. Several of them, in fact. You realize men can have and express deep emotions." As she spoke, she prayed for the right words to help Steele.

"Mike is all man."

"Exactly. And I'll bet he found the tears healing. Sometimes, maybe, to deny something inside us that God has put there is to tell God He made a mistake. And it robs us of being all God intended."

She shifted so she could watch his face and saw a play of emotions—doubt, stubborn refusal, acceptance, confusion. She thought of that little boy who had been Steele. "I think you have a very tender heart that you've been taught to deny. A little boy who likes pink flowers is the man who would rather pretend he hates them than have to face the hurt of that moment."

"I admit it. My feelings were hurt by Mom's remarks. I guess I got used to it. She loves me. Loves us all. But she thinks only tough feelings are masculine enough for her boys." He turned to face her, lifting his arm over the back of the seat to rest across her shoulders.

She tried not to miss the touch of their hands, the connection that had communicated his feelings even better than his words.

"It's all confusing, and I don't like the feeling. I want things to be sorted out. Cut and dried."

"Sometimes we have to take one step at a time, in faith, knowing God loves us and will show us what is best for us."

He cupped her cheek. "I wonder. What is best for us?"

"Us?" She could hardly get the word out past the sudden spasm of her lungs.

"A little surprising, maybe, but don't you think there's something between us? Something we should explore?"

Her lungs continued to draw inward as if guarding her surprise, her joy at his sudden realization and her own blaring truth. She loved this man who had just revealed a touching tenderness. Her love had been growing secretly day by day as he did sweet things for her that he would no doubt have called practical. She'd seen bits of romance in him, too, which served as rich nutrients to her emerging love. She forced her mouth to work. "I think there is definitely something that should be explored."

She leaned toward him, feeling so many things at once—a sorrow for the sad little boy, anger at the many years Steele had denied his real feelings, needing romance as much as she. Knowing it gave her the boldness to touch his cheek with her fingertips. His whiskers were rough beneath her hand. "Steele, you're a man with deep emotions both tough and tender. And they make you very appealing."

He needed no more invitation to pull her close and kiss her. She felt the answer of a lifetime of need and longing in this man who had admitted to hating pink flowers just because he liked them so much.

ten

The next couple of weeks were a delicious exploration of their relationship. They spent long hours walking and talking. Steele started showing up each day at closing time to help her push the planters and tables away. He took her to dinner and surprised her by choosing the most romantic place in town. On her part, Holly slipped over every day with a flower in a vase. She carefully avoided pink ones, sensing he still had some work to do in coming to grips with his feelings about them and all they signified for him. She knew he was changing but didn't want to push it. But she rejoiced to see him open up more and more about his feelings.

Nan and Henry had gone home.

"Are you two getting married?" Holly asked as Nan prepared to leave.

"We love each other, but we want to take our time. Not too much time, mind you. We aren't getting any younger. But there are some matters to take care of. Practical things."

Holly laughed as she told Steele. "There you go. Romantic and practical together."

There remained only one thing that stole from her happiness—her parents' continuing separation.

"Mom," she said, "Dad's trying hard. He's doing all the little things you like. Why don't you give him a chance?"

Her mother would only say, "I've gone too far to come back."

When Holly discussed it with Nan by phone, she voiced her confusion. "I don't understand. Dad's being romantic. Why isn't Mom accepting that?"

"Sometimes love needs more," Nan said. "Something else, like forgiveness."

"I'm sure Dad forgives her. After all, it wasn't like she committed the big sin."

"Maybe your mother needs to forgive herself. We will continue to pray for God to reach her heart and show her she's forgiven simply by confessing."

"She has to believe it. This can't be the end of their marriage."

But despite the bad, and the good, life went on.

She glanced up from giving a middle-aged couple a pink carnation and a card with the inscription by Martin Luther, "There is no more lovely, friendly, and charming relationship, communion, or company than a good marriage." She saw a man enter the building across the street. "No way," she muttered.

"Excuse me," the man at the table said.

"I'm sorry. I thought I saw my father go into that building." Out of loneliness, Holly supposed, her father had come to town to visit her.

"Then I expect he'll come over and have coffee with you when he's conducted his business."

"Of course." She moved away, putting a planter between herself and her customers, and stared across the street. Dad had met Steele on two occasions and voiced his admiration of him, but what business would he have over there? The light bounced off the dark glass of the windows of Steele's office. *No way.* But her insides froze into sharp, icy spears.

She pretended to be busy pruning the flowers and picking off dead leaves. Several times she washed the tables that allowed her a view of the street. Mostly she neglected her work for the next hour as she watched for her father to reappear. As the minutes ticked by, the icy spears melted with the dreaded suspicion that Dad would have only one reason to see Steele. She thought of the business he conducted there: divorce by request. But surely he wouldn't do that in this case. He'd send her father to a counselor, advise him to reconsider. Anything else was unthinkable. Yet, she knew it was part of his job. He only offered what any lawyer would. Still, she developed a slow simmer as she waited.

The minute her father stepped into view, she darted across the street, and barely missed being hit by a car.

"Dad!" she called.

He stopped, looked about as if wishing he could avoid this meeting.

"What were you doing in there?" She edged him toward the café as she talked. She'd serve him coffee with her inquisition, but she'd find out the truth.

"I spoke to Steele."

"About what?"

Dad sighed. "I guess you deserve the truth. I asked him to give your mother a speedy divorce."

She was thankful they had made it across the street, because Holly grabbed his arm and jerked him to a stop. "Dad, you can't be serious. You can't walk away from thirty years of marriage. Win her back. Romance her."

"Don't you think I've tried? It's not enough. I'm not enough. My love isn't enough. It's not fair for me to keep her tied to me when she's moved on in her heart."

Holly swallowed hard against the sudden nausea in her throat. "No way. You can't divorce. I won't let you." This couldn't be happening. Not to her parents. She believed in everlasting love. Hadn't they taught her love was for a lifetime? This was Steele's fault. "What did Steele say?" She ground out the words.

"He said I had a lot of things to take care of to ensure this didn't turn into a dirty fight. I told him I didn't care. Split everything down the middle. She deserves it. But it's a little hard to split a resort down the middle. One of us will have to buy out the other, I suppose. Or sell it to a third party."

Somehow Holly made her legs work and managed to sit down on a chair that felt as if someone had filled the seat with tiny tacks. She squeezed her knees together to stop her legs from shaking. "How can you even say that? It's my home."

Her father rubbed at his eyes. Peripherally, she noted how red rimmed they were, how he seemed to have aged twenty years. She forced herself to speak calmly, rationally, even though she could barely put together a coherent sentence.

"Dad, I can't believe there isn't some way to work things out. I'll talk to Mom again. Maybe if I invite her here, you could visit her."

"Honey, you can try. But don't be surprised if she refuses. I think she's having too much fun on her own."

"No, I think she's scared and alone and afraid to admit it. She keeps saying that what she did is so wrong, she's stepped beyond going back."

"I've tried to tell her it isn't so, but she doesn't hear me." The way he downed his coffee made her wonder that he didn't set his tongue on fire. Then he bolted to his feet. "I have to go. Steele insisted I make a list of all our assets."

Steele did, did he? He was actually encouraging her father in this? She struggled to her feet, waited for her legs to steady, then marched across the street and up the stairs to his office.

❧

Steele watched her head in his direction. Knew she'd be coming. But Glenn had asked for advice, and Steele couldn't refuse it. The man had too much to lose. Not just his marriage, which was devastating to everyone involved, but also his whole life's work and perhaps his retirement fund unless he had some good counsel to guide him through this. Not that Glenn cared. "Give it all to her," he'd said.

But one thing Steele had learned—when people were the most vulnerable, they made the worst choices and lived to regret them. They needed someone with a cool business head. That's where he came in.

Would Holly see this as part of his job, or would she take it personally?

She barged through the door before his secretary could end her message warning him, preparing him. He'd been preparing himself for the last twenty minutes, since Glenn left the office.

One look at her face, and he answered his own question. She would take it personally.

"How could you?" She breathed hard.

"Holly, have a chair. Let's talk reasonably."

"I don't want to sit." She leaned over the desk, eyeing him with all the feeling she'd give a bug crawling across her table. "You had the nerve to advise my father about a divorce? My father. This isn't someone coming in off the street, strangers or people who sit at the far side of the church. These are my parents. This affects me."

"I realize that. Which is why I want to make sure your father gets good advice and has some sound direction."

"Good advice? Did that include suggestions as to how he could mend things with my mother? The name of a good counselor?"

"Holly, that's not my expertise."

"Well, apparently my expertise doesn't include thinking you might have changed. How can I have anything to do with a man who is helping my father divorce my mother?" She took a step backward. "You don't believe in love."

"I believe in a love based on practical things, a love built on a solid foundation."

"I'm sorry. That's not the sort of love I need." She spun on her heel and left the room.

"Holly." He hurried after her, but she either didn't hear him or didn't care.

He returned to his office and stared out the window, watching as she returned to the café. She turned once to glower up at his windows then disappeared inside.

So that was that. Why should he be disappointed? Or surprised? He knew all that romance and lovey-dovey stuff didn't last. Had known it since he was knee-high to a grasshopper, as Pops would say. So why did he feel this terrible tightness in his chest, a stinging in his eyes?

Besides, who had said anything about love? Certainly not him.

Who was he kidding? No words had been spoken, but he knew without voicing the thought what was in his mind.

And he'd thought Holly's, as well.

He spun around and pulled out a stack of files. Men didn't cry. They worked.

By the end of the day, he was forced to admit that working got his desk cleared but didn't drive away the thought of Holly just a few steps away.

He stood at the windows, saw the empty flower cart. The day had almost ended. He could bury himself in work, but what would that get him? A clean desk. A harried secretary? Of course, he could always hire a second secretary, but that wouldn't solve what really bothered him.

He didn't want to lose Holly and this growing depth of feeling between them. He understood her anger and fear at her father's decision, but whether he came to Steele or went elsewhere, it shouldn't affect Holly and Steele's relationship. Surely she'd had time to realize that. He glanced at his watch. She'd soon be closing up. Indeed, she had already started carrying chairs inside.

He hurried out of his office and reached the café in time to grab the last two chairs from the sidewalk and carry them indoors.

They almost collided as she came through the door. "What are you doing here? Didn't I make it clear how angry I am with you?"

"You were pretty clear about it."

She stomped away.

"Your parents' problems aren't my fault, and you'd realize that if you gave yourself a chance." He pushed the planters inside and helped her drag in the tables. He waited until they'd done the chore before he poured them each a cup of coffee and led her to a table. "Holly, didn't you say at the banquet that you appreciated my practical help?"

"I did, and thank you for helping put the furniture inside."

He didn't want thanks. He wanted acknowledgment of what worked between them. "I've learned a lot from you. I might even be able to enjoy pink flowers now. Doesn't that mean anything to you?"

Her eyes softened. "I'm glad you are facing up to who you are—a blend of tough and tender."

He hoped for her to see the possibilities. But the corners of her mouth drew into tight lines, and he knew he had a long fight on his hands if he were to convince her.

She held her cup so tightly, her knuckles whitened. "But it isn't enough. There has to be more."

"What more? We could have a solid relationship built on mutual interests."

She rolled her eyes. "You sound like marriage is a contract."

"It is. A legal contract between a man and a woman."

"It's more than that. It's an emotional relationship."

"Granted. I thought we were achieving that." He fought his years of pushing away every soft and tender feeling, of hating romance, of scorning silly gestures. His parents didn't say the words of love. He'd learned, supposed, they weren't necessary. Knew the feeling without the words or acknowledgment. Now, when he wanted to say them, all those years of practicing not saying them stood in the way. He pushed through the habits, the teaching, the practice, and, yes, the fear. He found his way to the surface by focusing on Holly's face, seeing her sad, hurt eyes, remembering her sweetness and generosity. Surely she'd believe him if he brought the words out of the secret place inside him, the place that housed the scared little boy, the child crying over the pink flowers. "Holly, I think I might love you." He'd said it. Breathed the words that meant so much once spoken. It gave him a sudden rush of triumph, as if he'd reached the top of a steep slope and gained a view beyond words.

"Steele, I think I love you, too. That only makes this harder." She settled her gaze on the center of the table. "I don't know if it's enough. I don't want to end up like my mother—needing something for so long, so badly, that I ruin a marriage, a relationship, a family, and maybe even myself. I have to know that what we have is enough to satisfy me. I'm not sure it is." She pushed from the table, took their empty cups, and carried them to the sink behind the counter. "I have to be sure," she murmured before she turned on the water.

He followed her as far as the counter, leaned his elbows on it, and watched, waited, hoping for more. Hoping, he realized with such clarity he glanced overhead to see if she had somehow remotely flipped the lights on, that she'd do what she did best—believe in romance, fill his unfamiliar attempts with her bubbly optimism. Where were her verses and quotes of love now, when he was the one needing them?

Or was it she needing them? He knew no special verses, or he would offer them. *Love is. . .* He couldn't even remember the verses from the Bible he'd memorized in Sunday school.

She turned and faced him. "Steele, I need time to think. I need to work things out. Until I do, I think it's best if we don't see each other. Except when we can't avoid it like church, across the street. That sort of thing."

He searched her eyes, hoping for hesitation, regret, a change of heart. But her gaze had closed against him. He saw nothing but determined brown eyes.

"I'm sorry," she whispered. "I wish things could be different."

She turned away, returning to the hot water in the sink.

He backed out of the café and onto the sidewalk, where he stood staring about him, unable to think where to go next. Finally, with no destination in mind except to put his heart back the way it was before Holly had interfered, he strode down the street.

෨

Over the next few days, he buried himself in work, putting in longer hours than ever before. He dealt with a number of files he'd been neglecting, closed others with a few notes and the last bill.

He even agreed to represent the hotel across the street in dealing with a zoning bylaw. He usually avoided these meaningless legal wranglings. It kept him busy but was still boring enough to make his eyes water with stifled yawns.

On Saturday he persuaded Mike to go hiking with him in the mountains. Holly's parents owned a resort in the mountains. He wondered what it was like. From Glenn's list of assets, he guessed it was more than a couple of cabins and a gas station. And hadn't Holly mentioned movie stars staying there?

He increased his pace. Who needed to think about Holly? The sun was bright. The sky blue. The air pure. What else did a man need?

"Steele," Mike called. "Wait for me."

He realized he was panting from exertion. His legs quivered. He must be getting out of shape. He sat down and waited for Mike to join him.

"Trying to set a world record?" his brother demanded.

"Just working off energy."

Mike snorted. "Never seen you so angry."

"I'm not angry." He kept his voice supremely calm.

"Yeah. Tell that to someone who might believe you. Wouldn't have anything to do with Holly? I hear tell you two are on the outs."

"We found we want different things in life."

"Care to talk about it?"

"Let me think." He pushed to his feet. "No." He rushed up the trail, not caring that Mike was left behind. He reached the summit and sat down to enjoy the view. *Enjoy,* he ordered himself. As far as a man could see, not a sign of another human. Could make a man feel mighty lonely if he was given to such emotional nonsense. Steele wasn't. It was a wonderful view. Worth the climb.

Mike caught up and plunked down on the ground beside Steele, panting hard. "You can't outrun your feelings, you know."

"Who's running? Not me." He forced himself to remain seated, calmly looking out over the scene.

"For a smart lawyer, you can be mighty dumb."

Steele didn't answer. Lately he'd been feeling dumb all right. Why had he let Holly sweet-talk him into thinking they had something in common? Why had he shared that stupid story about crying over pink flowers? Mom was right. Flowers were silly, and a man could make a fool of himself over a woman. He didn't have to look farther than the mirror to know the truth of that statement.

&

His days blended into a steady stream of work. He allowed himself to think of nothing else. He avoided the windows of his office, but unbidden his gaze went to the spot on his desk where Holly had daily put a flower in a tiny crystal vase. He did not miss the flower. And he'd get used to not seeing her.

The phone rang, and he answered it.

"Hi there, young man. How are you doing?"

"Fine, Grandpops. Are you keeping out of trouble?"

"No fun in that now, is there?"

Steele leaned back, trying to remember how this exchange used to amuse him.

"How's that little Holly girl?"

"Fine."

"That's not the way I hear it. Jean says she's moping."

"She's worried about her parents' marriage." He ignored Pops's grunt of disbelief. If Holly had any other reason to be unhappy, it was not his doing. It was hers. She'd been the one to close the door between them.

"So how are things with you and Jean?" Surefire way to get Pops to leave him alone.

"Couldn't be better." He chuckled heartily. "The old sweetie has agreed to marry me."

Steele stilled his objections, knowing they were based on something from his childhood. "Glad for both of you."

"There's lots to consider for an old pair like us. We've both been to see our lawyers and signed papers and stuff. But I want to make sure I've done it all right. That's where having a lawyer in the family comes in handy. We signed prenups keeping all the inheritances in each family as they should be. I set up a fund for her in case something should happen to me. She didn't much care for that. Said she had plenty of her own to live on."

After a few minutes, Steele admitted Grandpops had

taken care of everything in a very efficient manner. "Here I was afraid you'd let all that romantic nonsense and memories of being young and fancy-free affect your good sense."

"Boy, it's possible to have both romance and practicality. Maybe that's what you need to learn. Seems all my girling lessons failed to take on you. You're not such a good student."

Steele ignored the undeserved jibe. "Maybe you're not such a good teacher."

"Whatever you did to that little gal, it's time you swallowed your pride and fixed it."

Sounded easy coming from Pops's mouth.

"Steele, you have what that girl needs. Now go convince her of it. By the way, Jean and I are planning an engagement party for next Saturday. We decided to have it in Missoula as sort of a central place. We expect all the family to be in attendance."

It wasn't even offered as an invite. It was an order if he'd ever heard one, and no one ignored his grandfather's orders unless they wanted to deal with an irate old man.

"I'll be there to congratulate you both."

He stared at the phone long after he'd hung up, Pops's words circling in his head. *You have what that girl needs.* How could Pops think such a thing? Holly wasn't convinced. Steele sure wasn't.

Go convince her.

First he had to convince himself.

eleven

When Nan asked to stay with Holly and wanted her to help plan the engagement party, Holly had mixed feelings. She couldn't get enthused about all the flowers and candles, but she couldn't refuse Nan. Any more than her parents would be able to. Whether they wanted to see each other or not, she doubted either would have a sufficient excuse to miss the party. Nan might accept an absence if one of them were in ICU, but she could think of nothing short of that her grandmother would consider reason enough to miss this event.

Even though Holly understood she would have to face Steele, which filled her heart with a queer mixture of anticipation and dread, she looked forward to the chance to see her parents together in the same room. This might be the answer to her prayers as a way to get her parents back together.

When they each protested they couldn't come, Holly just laughed. "I'll let you explain that to Nan yourself." Neither of them had pursued the topic further.

The best part of the whole thing, though, was working with Nan. She saw a side of her grandmother she'd never before seen. An efficient, hard-driving side that rented a hall in Missoula and saw things got done according to her wishes and on her time schedule.

And now the day of the party had arrived. Holly and Nan planned to spend the afternoon preparing.

"Where do you want the flowers?" Holly asked.

"Everywhere. I want the whole room to breathe perfume."

"That would explain the scented candles in this box. Sure hope no one is allergic to scents."

"If anyone complains, we'll put the candles out. So what's happening between you and Steele?"

"Nothing, Nan. I told you. We just don't fit together."

Nan put a large bouquet in the center of the head table then turned and took Holly's hands. "Child, do you love him?"

Holly nodded. "Unwisely, yes."

Nan chuckled softly. "When is love wise?"

"I have been praying I can forget him." Saying the words felt like acid on her soul.

"Holly, sweetie, are you sure that's what you want? Or are you just afraid to take a risk? Look at Henry and me and see what happens when you're afraid of risks."

"But look at Mom and Dad. They married, and they discovered they couldn't get what they needed in a marriage."

"I admit your parents are going through a rough time, but I know they'll be okay. And maybe marriage isn't about getting what we need as much as it is about loving someone enough to see they get what they need. Meeting their emotional needs becomes our emotional need."

Nan's statement made Holly realize how small and selfish her desires were. And yet. . .

Nan continued. "Love is so many things. It's being romantic; it's being practical. It's speaking kind words. It's forgiving the unkind ones. It's changing the baby, fixing a tire, mowing the lawn, holding hands, holding a basin while someone is sick. People need different things at different times, and that's what real love is. Doing what the person you love needs at the moment."

Tears stung Holly's eyes. "Nan, that is beautiful. You should make it your wedding vows."

"Maybe I will, but right now I want to know, do you love Steele enough to meet his needs? If not, maybe you don't love him enough."

Nan turned back to the flowers and left Holly to consider her words. How much did she love Steele? Enough to be practical? She smiled, thinking of how she'd learned to be just that in the past few weeks. In little ways she'd hardly noticed—fixing Steele his favorite sandwich, applying a bandage when he scraped his knuckles bringing in a table. She'd seen it as romantic, but it was practical, too.

How could she be sure? She didn't want to end up like so many couples, visiting lawyers, begging for a divorce. Or stuck in a relationship that left her empty and unsatisfied.

Could she trust a man who would help her parents get a divorce?

She had to know what was right. She didn't want to make a mistake. Too many people could be hurt. She'd seen how devastated her father was by his marriage problems. She knew her mother's pain, had listened to her cry and been powerless to do anything. *Dear God, please help my parents find a way back together, and show me what's best for me.*

❧

Nan was beautiful in a beige suit with a corsage of red, red roses pinned to her jacket. Beside her, in his black suit with a red rose boutonniere, Henry looked as handsome and proud as a gold medal winner on a podium.

Holly held her father's arm. "Don't they look nice together?"

Dad nodded. "I'm glad for my mother. I just wish. . ."

"Me, too."

"Is your mother coming?"

"She said she was. Nan ordered it, you know. Don't think that leaves much room for excuses."

They chuckled together, sharing the knowledge that family members didn't disobey a directive from Grandmother Hope.

But Holly wondered if Mom would show. She allowed herself a glance around the room, telling herself she was only checking to see if Mom had slipped in. But it wasn't Mom her gaze sought. It was Steele.

He wore a casual gray blazer and dark pants. His white shirt lay open at the neck, emphasizing his summer tan. His hair had lightened. He must be spending time outdoors.

She was glad. He should enjoy the lovely weather.

He turned. Their gazes collided.

Even from this distance, she jolted from the demanding power in his eyes. Her knees began to wilt like yesterday's flowers. She loved him. She ached to be able to give him what he needed. But she was her mother's daughter in so many ways. She would walk away right now rather than risk hurting Steele farther down the road, as her mother was hurting her father with her hunger for romance.

Steele pulled a rose from the bouquet in front of him and lifted it to her.

She jerked away. What did that gesture mean? Was he saying she must be happy to see all these flowers and feel the romance that filled the room as much as the scent of candles and roses? She was happy, but not for the flowers and scents. Rather she was happy for the love Nan and Henry had rediscovered. She'd have been just as happy in a tiny hall without a decoration or flower in sight or huddled around the kitchen table if it allowed her to share this moment.

She saw a movement at the doorway. "Dad, Mom just came in."

"Holly, she looks lost and scared." He took a step toward her, stopped. "She doesn't want to see me." He turned back to Holly, his face so filled with sorrow that she grabbed his shoulders and hugged him.

His words strangled, he said, "Go to your mother and make sure she's all right."

She studied his face, saw the tears on his cheeks. "Oh, Dad. This is just so wrong."

"I wish your mother agreed." He tried to smile but failed miserably.

Holly glanced over his shoulder to her mother, wanted to go to her, but didn't want to abandon her father. "Will you be okay if I leave?"

"I'll never be okay again." He gave her a little shove. "Go to her."

Holly crossed the room, felt Steele's gaze as she passed him, but carefully avoided glancing in his direction.

"Mom, I'm glad you made it." She hugged her mother and felt the tension in her, which made Holly hold her gently for fear of breaking something. Her mother had lost weight. Her eyes lacked their usual sparkle, and yet she was still beautiful in her royal blue dress.

"I shouldn't have come. I don't belong here."

"Of course you do. You're part of the family."

"Things have changed."

Holly held back the words crowding her mind. *Yes, Mom, they have. And you're the only one who can put them back together.* "Mom, I wish you'd give Dad a chance."

"Let's not talk about that. I'm finding it hard enough to

stay here without having to face my guilt."

Holly couldn't let it go. "Mom, didn't you teach me there is a remedy for guilt?"

Mom turned her startled gaze toward Holly.

"You said there is nothing God can't forgive. Nothing. I remember how you emphasized that word."

Mom's surprised expression turned into stubbornness. "It's not that easy. Sin has a consequence."

"For which, if I remember the Bible correctly, Jesus died. Again it was you who taught me the words in John 8:36." She grinned triumphantly. "See, I even remember where it's found." She was rewarded with a fleeting smile from her mother. " 'So if the Son sets you free, you will be free indeed.' " Her voice fell to a hoarse whisper. "I remember the day you taught me that verse. I had done something really bad, and I was miserable about it. We were visiting Nan, and I had stolen raspberries from the neighbor's bushes. I was so filled with guilt. It was you who said I had done wrong and I needed to apologize for it. You said one must always do what they could to make up for wrongdoings. You went with me to speak to the neighbor." She wrapped her arm around her mother's thin waist. "I don't remember what she said, but I remember as clearly as if it were today what you said. 'Use this as a lesson to never repeat the sin, but move on from here knowing God has forgiven you.' "

Her mother shuddered twice, as if holding back sobs.

"Mom, maybe you should follow your own advice."

She turned to Holly, her eyes watery. "If only—"

At the front of the hall, Henry cleared his throat. "Folks!" he roared and instantly had everyone's attention.

Holly held her mother's elbow. "What?" She wanted to

know what Mom had been about to say.

Mom shook her head and turned her gaze toward the front of the room, where Henry and Nan stood.

Holly swallowed her disappointment. *If only what? Why couldn't Henry have waited two more minutes?* She sucked in a deep breath. It was a start. *Lord, help Mom be willing to believe in Your forgiveness.*

Henry held up his hand. "I expect you all know why you're here, but allow me to do the honors." He reached for Nan's hand and pulled her to his side. "Jean has generously agreed to marry this old goat of a man. She has given me joy I never expected to have again. We haven't set a date yet, but it will be soon. We haven't near enough time left to enjoy each other."

People laughed.

"Now that our two families are to be joined, I think we need to make introductions."

Mom jerked as if she'd been jump-started with electric paddles. She stepped away from Holly and darted a glance to the door.

"I have to leave," she whispered.

"Not until you are introduced as my mother." Holly grabbed her hand and refused to release her.

Henry called Steele's parents up. "My son and daughter-in-law, John and Justine."

Holly studied the couple. The man wore jeans and a button-front, open-necked denim blue shirt. He had the rugged appearance of a man who worked outdoors, made his living doing physical work.

Steele's mother wore black jeans and a shirt much like her husband's in a softer shade of blue. She shared a similar rugged appearance. But the look they gave each other spoke of mutual love and care.

Nan kissed each of them on the cheek then turned to her son. "Glenn." She held out one hand to Holly's father. "Karen." She held out the other to Holly's mom.

Holly urged her mother forward, one painfully slow step at a time. She stood back as soon as Nan took Mom's hand. Her grandmother quirked her eyebrow, and Holly knew Mom would not be escaping Nan's firm grasp until Nan decided it was time.

"My son and daughter-in-law," Nan announced.

Henry kissed Mom on the cheek and shook hands with Dad. "You did a fine job of raising Jean," he said. Everyone but Mom laughed.

Steele's parents shook hands with Holly's parents.

"My grandsons," Henry boomed. "Mike, Steele, and Billy-boy."

Holly chuckled as a young man groaned. Apparently Bill didn't care for his grandfather's nickname. She smiled at Mike, skipped past Steele, and smiled at Bill as he took his place in the family lineup.

"Three strapping young men and none of them married. Can you believe it? Where did I fail?"

More laughter. Holly giggled as the three young men groaned.

Nan beckoned to Holly. "My one and only grandchild."

Holly moved to stand at her mother's side, took her hand, let her squeeze as hard as she wanted.

Nan smiled at Henry. "I'm dreaming of a whole bunch of great-grandchildren."

He chortled. "At the rate this bunch of ours is going, you

might have a long wait."

Holly wouldn't look at Steele to see his reaction to all this good-natured teasing. Just a quick glimpse to see if he found it amusing or annoying.

A jolt raced through her when their gazes connected. She felt Mom glance at her, aware of the way Holly had jerked. She couldn't tear her gaze away from Steele's to assure Mom everything was okay.

A sudden, terrible, lovely truth filled her.

Not only did she love him, but he'd given her everything she needed. Maybe he'd get over his pink phobia. Maybe he wouldn't. It didn't matter. She knew his tender side. Had felt his pain at rejecting his inner needs. Knew he ached for the words and gestures she would willingly give.

Mom squeezed her hand hard enough to make her fingers hurt.

Holly knew how much she and her mother were alike. Would she hurt Steele with her needs and demands? It was a risk she couldn't take. But how could she live without him? Again she prayed for wisdom and guidance.

Henry spoke. "I want you all to be friends. Now help yourself to coffee and tea. Enjoy the cakes and sandwiches. Most of all, enjoy visiting."

Mom broke free and with stiff dignity walked to the back of the room.

Holly grabbed coffee and snacks, hurried after her, and persuaded her to sit. She knew the strain was taking its toll and feared her mother would faint.

As she sat beside her, she watched Steele and her dad talking. Was he counseling her father about a divorce? She wanted to trust Steele, but this aspect of his work bothered her. She did not believe divorce was the answer for troubled marriages.

Mike approached her, and she rose to speak to him.

"You're the girl who came with Steele to rescue me a few weeks ago. Thank you."

"I didn't do anything." She studied him. Liked his loose-limbed casualness. "How are you doing?"

"Better. I guess each day gets a little better, though it will never be the same as before, if you know what I mean."

"I can only understand from my perspective." Experiencing the idea of divorce through her parents hurt bad enough. She couldn't imagine Mike's pain. Or how he dealt with it.

She shifted to check on Mom. She wasn't there. She stood near the door, talking to Steele. First Dad and now Mom. This then was God's direction. She couldn't trust a man who counseled her parents about divorce. How dare he?

Mom nodded at whatever he said and moved away.

"Excuse me." She left Mike in midsentence and headed for Steele. He must have seen the anger on her face, for he backed away at her approach.

"I do not want my parents to divorce," she spat out. "Don't be telling them the best way to do it."

He gave a smug smile. "Hello, Holly, how are you? Nice get-together for the grandparents. I hope they'll be very happy."

She faltered. "Steele, why do you have to make it possible for people to get a divorce?"

"I am not responsible for marriage breakdown."

"I know that."

"I see my job being to protect people when they're too vulnerable to make sound choices. They have to live with their decisions long after the papers are signed. And there are often children to consider."

She hesitated. He made it sound so logical. But it was personal when it came to her parents. Too confused to know what to say, she turned, saw her mother across the room, and went to join her.

"Do you know what Steele just offered me—us?" Mom said, sounding surprised, almost hopeful.

"No." She didn't want to know. She didn't want to deal with this aspect of Steele. Yes, it was his work. But it hurt her somewhere deep inside to think of his helping people end their marriages. Marriages, he pointed out, that were already over. Suddenly she had an insight into his thinking. His concern was protecting the people involved. She gave a little laugh.

Mom sent her a startled look. "What's so funny?"

"Sorry, Mom. I was thinking of something else." Maybe she could live with this part of his work if she just kept in mind how he'd explained it. "What did Steele say to you?"

"He said he thought what your father and I had was too precious to throw away. He offered to pay for some marriage counseling and a weekend in a resort near Seattle. He said if we both felt the same way afterward, he would then help us with the divorce and property settlement."

Holly massaged her chest as if she could stop the pain by the action. She'd been so wrong about Steele. She grabbed her mother's arms. "You're going to take him up on his offer, aren't you?"

Mom sniffed. "I don't know."

Holly continued to rub her chest. "I've made a really stupid mistake." She told how she'd misjudged Steele.

"It was an understandable mistake. Forgive yourself," Mom said.

"It's not easy, is it?"

Doubt returned to her mother's eyes.

"I'll tell you what. I'll forgive myself if you forgive yourself."

Mom allowed hope to enter her eyes then shook her head. Suddenly she smiled, taking ten years off her face. "I guess I have to practice what I preach. I think you and I are a lot alike. Holly, honey, we can't afford to overlook the love that's right under our noses." Mom patted Holly's arm. "Now if you'll excuse me, I am going to talk to your father. Steele's right. We need to give our marriage another chance."

Holly watched Mom through a haze of tears. She dashed them away so she could see the love and relief on Dad's face when Mom spoke to him. *Thank You, Lord. Thank You.*

Maybe being her mother's daughter wasn't something to fear but to embrace.

Her father gave Holly a thumbs-up sign.

It was a beginning. A new beginning for them.

She looked around for Steele and found him standing with his brothers. She gathered up her courage and headed in his direction, but before she crossed the room, the three of them hurried outside. She rushed after them and reached the door in time to see them drive away in Steele's SUV.

For a long time, she stared after them.

She had no one but herself to blame that he couldn't wait to get away from her. She'd hurt him so many times. She vowed she'd never hurt him again. *With Your help, God.* She wanted to share his joys, halve his sorrows, but never again hurt him. His mother had done so in the past through her own strong character. Out of ignorance, Holly was sure. But Holly wanted to spend the rest of her life nurturing his gentle side while enjoying his practical side.

She remembered Nan's words. "It's about loving someone enough to see they get what they need. Meeting their emotional needs becomes our emotional need."

She smiled into the now-empty street, seeing Steele's gestures—filling her coffee cup, pushing in the planters. A unique combination of romantic and practical.

"The boys left, did they?"

Holly turned to acknowledge Steele's mother. "Yes."

The woman studied her openly. "So our families are to be united."

Holly felt hot embarrassment rush up her neck, thinking the woman read her thoughts, startled to realize she'd been thinking marriage to Steele. Then her mind kicked into gear. "Nan and Henry. Yes."

"Henry is a nice man."

"Nan's a nice woman."

"I'm sure she is, or he wouldn't be marrying her."

Their conversation felt like a duel of words. She welcomed the relief when the woman looked down the street again.

"Steele is like Henry." She sounded more exasperated than proud. "A strange combination of hardness and softness. I never did know how to handle him. Now the other two, they're not so complicated. Give them some good hard work, and they're happy."

Although the other woman sounded frustrated, her words filled Holly with growing assurance that Steele was exactly the sort of man she needed and wanted.

But how to make up for all her mistakes and prove to him what was in her heart, buried for a time beneath doubts and fears?

Steele's father joined them, draping his arm across his wife's shoulders. "What are the boys up to?"

Mrs. Davis smiled. "They've gone to pick up something for Grandpops."

Holly excused herself and returned to the party although she felt little party spirit. Even the return of Steele and his brothers didn't give her cause to celebrate. They delivered a parcel to the front. Henry quietly presented it to Nan. She unwrapped it and laughed then threw her arms around Henry's neck.

Henry held the gift for all to see. Holly's eyes blurred when she saw it was a painting of Henry and Nan together at the picnic she and Steele had gone on with them. Henry must have had it painted from the photo Holly had taken that day. And it would explain why Henry had begged it off her and made her promise not to mention it to Nan.

Afterward, the three brothers moved around the room as a unit, making it impossible for her to apologize to Steele. She overheard him tell his mother he and his brothers planned to spend the weekend hiking in the mountains.

She'd have to wait until his return to speak to him.

⁂

Steele returned from a vigorous weekend. His brothers might be into physical work on a daily basis, but he had left them panting and begging him to slow down.

Mike had waited until they huddled around the fireplace roasting wieners and burning marshmallows before he started his free analysis of Steele's psyche. "You can't get away from your feelings, man. Take it from someone who knows."

"Sounds to me like you're about to make excuses for not being able to keep up. Maybe your age is starting to show."

He loved to rub in the fact Mike was a year older. "So what's your excuse, Billy-boy?"

The youngest brother laughed. "Leave me out of this argument. Trouble with you two is you let yourself care too much about one woman. Take me. I know how to enjoy them without getting all tangled up inside."

Mike understood too much of how Steele was feeling, though Steele would never give him the satisfaction of admitting it. He'd spent two days trying to drive Holly from his thoughts with physical exercise, but sore muscles were all he'd managed to achieve.

She'd made it clear at the engagement party that she would never trust him. She hadn't even given him a chance to explain. Later, he'd avoided her. Didn't want to hear any more accusations. He just wanted to forget her.

But Mike was right. There seemed no way to run from his feelings. Feelings he didn't intend to validate by naming.

જ

Steele sat behind his desk staring at the pile of work before him. His secretary knocked. "Delivery for you, Steele." She placed a parcel on his desk and retreated.

He turned the package around with little interest. He hadn't ordered anything and didn't much care for unsolicited freebies. But it beat tackling the files on his desk, so he ripped it open. Inside sat a foil-wrapped parcel and an envelope.

He slid his thumbnail under the flap of the envelope and pulled out a card. His thoughts stalled as he saw a construction scene with piles of dirt and rough ground with a big yellow Cat in the back. Right dead center in the foreground sat a tiny green wrought-iron bistro table and two people with their hands clasped. The man, his back showing, wore a suit and a bright yellow hard hat. No mistaking the caricature of the woman. A mass of waves, big brown eyes. Really big. Surrounding the table, cutting them off from the construction scene, banks and banks of purple flowers.

He traced his fingertip over the flowers, rested it on the face of the woman. A smile tugged at his heart, crept to his mouth. Holly—sweet, romantic and idealistic—had sent him a card she'd painted. He wasn't sure what it meant except it promised better things ahead.

He flipped open the card and read the verse inside, penned in precise calligraphy:

Love is a many splendored thing.
It is different for different people,
Different things at different times.

Beneath it she had written, *Steele, I'm sorry. Can you give me another chance?*

Men don't cry. They don't get all mushy about flowers and cards. He'd been told so all his life. Yet he'd never believed it. Not really. And he certainly didn't at this moment as his vision blurred. He knew what this card meant. It was more than an apology. It was an invitation. Acceptance. By putting the flowers and table in the center of a construction site, she'd informed him that their very different viewpoints worked together in a way unique to them.

He hurried over to the windows and stared down at the café, hoping to see her giving out flowers and optimism. He wasn't disappointed. She bent toward a couple at a table tucked between two planter dividers, placing a pink flower in the center of the table and then spun away, her hair cascading about her shoulders as she turned. In his mind, he heard her laughing.

He grabbed the phone and made arrangements for a special

delivery. Only then did he reach for the unopened gift and pulled out a tiny crystal vase. It held a purple gerbera daisy in water. How had it managed not to spill? He tipped it slightly. It wasn't water, just some kind of gel that looked like water. He laughed out loud and put the vase in the center front of his desk where he sat and stared at it.

The clock moved toward closing time with agonizing slowness. Finally the hour arrived, and he hurried across the street, carrying the card and gift with him.

She saw him, stopped, and waited, her eyes almost as wide as on the card. He sensed her uncertainty in the way she squeezed the tea towel in her hands until her knuckles looked like a row of white marbles.

"Thanks for the gift." He held out the vase. "And a very nice card."

"You like them?" Her voice quavered uncertainly.

He longed to ease her concerns but knew it wasn't as simple as pulling her into his arms and kissing her. They had to resolve some of the issues between them. "I do. Especially the card. Did you mean to show us working things out?"

She nodded. "Is it possible?"

He turned her toward a table and called for Meggie to bring them coffee. "I think it's very possible. What we are is a little bit romantic, a little bit practical. We have our own unique blend. A balance maybe."

"Nan said we balanced each other." Holly chuckled. "She seemed to think that was a good thing."

He traced the line of her jaw with his finger, paused to play with a strand of hair, letting himself love everything about this woman from her wavy hair, to her uncertain smile, to her romantic idealism. "Holly, for the first time since I was a little kid, I feel satisfied about who I am. I've been hiding my true feelings about a lot of things behind my defense of practical. But the closer I get to you, the more comfortable I am acknowledging who I really am and what I want."

Her eyes filled with the light of a thousand stars. "That's wonderful. I'm glad." She pressed her hand over his, capturing it against her cheek. "In you I've found what I need and want. I've found solidness that allows me to trust as much as I dream. I trust you. I know I haven't exactly shown it, but I've been afraid." She turned and placed a kiss in his palm.

Her confession puzzled him. "What are you afraid of?"

She lifted a shy look to him. "Hurting you like Mom hurt Dad. I don't know that I can be all you need."

His words scratched from a throat that tightened at her confession. "No one has ever cared about what I need like you do. Holly, we'll both make mistakes. Only God is perfect. As long as we stay close to Him, He'll enable us to overcome our weaknesses, to grow and to forgive each other and ourselves when we need it."

"I like that," she whispered.

He forced himself to ignore the way she looked at him, all kissable and eager. "Holly, I've done some serious soul searching about what I believe—really believe—about love and marriage. Not just the words but where the rubber meets the road. Right in my office. I still want to help people so they don't make momentous mistakes at a time when they are thinking with their emotions. But in the future, I'll only act to protect a marriage."

Tears spilled from her eyes.

He grabbed a napkin and dabbed at them, his heart ready to burst from the pain of making her cry. "I thought you'd be happy about it."

"I am. These are happy tears."

"Whew. You scared me."

"Steele Davis, you are a generous and kind man. I'm so proud to know you."

At that moment, the delivery van pulled up. Two men got out carrying armloads of pink carnations. They filled Holly's arms and her lap. Several times they returned to the van for more flowers. They piled them on the table, arranged vases of them on the floor around Holly, and put more on the adjoining table.

Steele handed them a tip, grinning at Holly's surprise.

"What is this?"

"I'm setting the scene." Every pain of rejected, denied emotions of his past was washed away by the look in her darkening eyes, full of expectant trust. He would spend the rest of his life fulfilling that trust if she'd let him.

He went to her side, fell to one knee, and took her hand. "Holly Hope, I love you. I want to spend the rest of my life doing my best to make you happy. Will you marry me and let me do that?"

"I love you, Steele Davis. I'd be honored to marry you. And I promise to spend the rest of my life doing my best to satisfy your needs."

Ignoring the pink flowers that almost buried her, he cupped her head and kissed her with a heart full of love and gratitude.

When he finally released her, her cheeks glowed the color of the flowers. Her eyes glistened with some sort of inner joy.

She gave a long look around. "Pink flowers?"

He nodded. "Can't think of a better way to say 'I love you.'"

epilogue

Holly's mother smiled as she adjusted Holly's veil. "You're the most beautiful bride."

Nan chuckled. "What does that make me?"

Holly and Mom laughed and shared a special glance of understanding. "You're beautiful, too," they chorused. Indeed, Nan, in a slim-fitting, pink silk suit, glowed like a summer sky just as the sun teased at the horizon. Holly knew the glow had nothing to do with the color of Nan's suit. It came from inside. She knew because her own insides glowed so warm she thought her heart would spontaneously combust.

Mom hurried to peek through the doors. For the seven hundredth time. As if she were the one getting married. "Isn't it time to begin? When's the organist going to start our song?"

Nan and Holly smiled at each other at Mom's impatience.

"You're sure you don't mind sharing your day with an old lady?" Nan asked, marring her serenity with a tiny frown.

"Not one bit. I'm glad we decided to do this together," Holly whispered, her throat tightening. "It makes the day even more special."

The music changed.

"About time," Mom grumbled. She backed from the door. "Do I look okay?"

"Mom, you're beautiful." She wore a frothy dress in pale

blue. She'd gained back the weight she'd lost. "You could pass for my sister. Now go."

Mom drew in a deep breath and marched down the aisle.

Nan was next. She never faltered. Never hesitated. Didn't even glance back at Holly.

And then it was Holly's turn. Dad joined her. "You ready, my sweet daughter?"

"Are you ready, my handsome father?"

He grinned. "Let's do this."

Holly stepped into the church, forced herself to look at Mom waiting at the front, Nan and Henry beside her, and then allowed herself to meet Steele's gaze. After that, nothing else mattered. If not for Dad's steadying arm, she would have raced to Steele's side.

"Who giveth this woman?" Pastor Don asked.

Dad handed her to Steele then took his place beside Mom.

Pastor Don addressed the gathered friends and family.

"Today we are witnesses of a unique ceremony. The marriage of Steele and Holly. The marriage of their grandparents. And the renewal of vows between Holly's parents. A blessed occasion, indeed."

Mom and Dad renewed their vows. Holly had promised herself she wouldn't cry, and she succeeded, though it took a few deep breaths. Steele squeezed her hand. She knew he understood her emotion at seeing her parents recommit to each other. She had him to thank for helping them.

Then Nan and Henry exchanged vows. Holly pressed her lips together and widened her eyes. She would not cry on her wedding day no matter how touched she was by the deep, open love between the older couple.

And then it was their turn. She turned to face Steele and almost lost control of her tears when she saw how his eyes glistened. She loved him all the more for his tender side.

They promised to love each other until death. Then the three couples moved to sign the register, Mom and Dad witnessing both marriages.

She glanced about. Love was truly a unique thing for each couple. The grandparents, a blend of romance and practicality. Her parents, a love based on hope and forgiveness. Steele's parents, their love so practical, yet for them exactly what they needed and wanted.

She glanced up at Steele, her new husband. Their love was a blend of all of the above. It would change and grow as they did.

The pastor asked the congregation to stand as he prayed.

"Lord, bless these unions with enduring marriages and everlasting love. Amen."

The six people at the front echoed with a resounding "Amen."

A Letter To Our Readers

Dear Reader:
In order that we might better contribute to your reading enjoyment, we would appreciate your taking a few minutes to respond to the following questions. We welcome your comments and read each form and letter we receive. When completed, please return to the following:

Fiction Editor
Heartsong Presents
PO Box 719
Uhrichsville, Ohio 44683

1. Did you enjoy reading *Everlasting Love* by Linda Ford?
   ❏ Very much! I would like to see more books by this author!
   ❏ Moderately. I would have enjoyed it more if

   _____
   _____
   _____

2. Are you a member of **Heartsong Presents**?   ❏ Yes   ❏ No
   If no, where did you purchase this book? _____
   _____

3. How would you rate, on a scale from 1 (poor) to 5 (superior), the cover design? _____

4. On a scale from 1 (poor) to 10 (superior), please rate the following elements.

   ____ Heroine   ____ Plot
   ____ Hero   ____ Inspirational theme
   ____ Setting   ____ Secondary characters

5. These characters were special because? _____

_____

_____

6. How has this book inspired your life? _____

_____

_____

7. What settings would you like to see covered in future
   Heartsong Presents books? _____

_____

_____

8. What are some inspirational themes you would like to see
   treated in future books? _____

_____

_____

9. Would you be interested in reading other **Heartsong
   Presents** titles?   ❏ Yes   ❏ No

10. Please check your age range:
    ❏ Under 18   ❏ 18-24
    ❏ 25-34   ❏ 35-45
    ❏ 46-55   ❏ Over 55

Name_____

Occupation _____

Address _____

City, State, Zip_____

RHODE ISLAND
Weddings

3 stories in 1

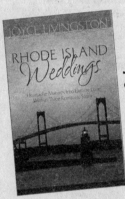

Join three Rhode Island couples as they work to strengthen their love in the midst of personal trials.

Contemporary, paperback, 352 pages, 5³⁄₁₆" x 8"

Hearts♥ng

Any 12 Heartsong Presents titles for only $27.00*

CONTEMPORARY ROMANCE IS CHEAPER BY THE DOZEN!

Buy any assortment of twelve *Heartsong Presents* titles and save 25% off the already discounted price of $2.97 each!

*plus $3.00 shipping and handling per order and sales tax where applicable. If outside the U.S. please call 740-922-7280 for shipping charges.

HEARTSONG PRESENTS TITLES AVAILABLE NOW:

___HP501 *The Thrill of the Hunt*, T. H. Murray
___HP502 *Whole in One*, A. Ford
___HP505 *Happily Ever After*, M. Panagiotopoulos
___HP506 *Cords of Love*, L. A. Coleman
___HP509 *His Christmas Angel*, G. Sattler
___HP510 *Past the Ps Please*, Y. Lehman
___HP513 *Licorice Kisses*, D. Mills
___HP514 *Roger's Return*, M. Davis
___HP517 *The Neighborly Thing to Do*, W. E. Brunstetter
___HP518 *For a Father's Love*, J. A. Grote
___HP521 *Be My Valentine*, J. Livingston
___HP522 *Angel's Roost*, J. Spaeth
___HP525 *Game of Pretend*, J. Odell
___HP526 *In Search of Love*, C. Lynxwiler
___HP529 *Major League Dad*, K. Y'Barbo
___HP530 *Joe's Diner*, G. Sattler
___HP533 *On a Clear Day*, Y. Lehman
___HP534 *Term of Love*, M. Pittman Crane
___HP537 *Close Enough to Perfect*, T. Fowler
___HP538 *A Storybook Finish*, L. Bliss
___HP541 *The Summer Girl*, A. Boeshaar
___HP542 *Clowning Around*, W. E. Brunstetter
___HP545 *Love Is Patient*, C. M. Hake
___HP546 *Love Is Kind*, J. Livingston
___HP549 *Patchwork and Politics*, C. Lynxwiler
___HP550 *Woodhaven Acres*, B. Etchison
___HP553 *Bay Island*, B. Loughner
___HP554 *A Donut a Day*, G. Sattler
___HP557 *If You Please*, T. Davis
___HP558 *A Fairy Tale Romance*, M. Panagiotopoulos
___HP561 *Ton's Vow*, K. Cornelius
___HP562 *Family Ties*, J. L. Barton
___HP565 *An Unbreakable Hope*, K. Billerbeck
___HP566 *The Baby Quilt*, J. Livingston
___HP569 *Ageless Love*, L. Bliss
___HP570 *Beguiling Masquerade*, C. G. Page

___HP573 *In a Land Far Far Away*, M. Panagiotopoulos
___HP574 *Lambert's Pride*, L. A. Coleman and R. Hauck
___HP577 *Anita's Fortune*, K. Cornelius
___HP578 *The Birthday Wish*, J. Livingston
___HP581 *Love Online*, K. Billerbeck
___HP582 *The Long Ride Home*, A. Boeshaar
___HP585 *Compassion's Charm*, D. Mills
___HP586 *A Single Rose*, P. Griffin
___HP589 *Changing Seasons*, C. Reece and J. Reece-Demarco
___HP590 *Secret Admirer*, G. Sattler
___HP593 *Angel Incognito*, J. Thompson
___HP594 *Out on a Limb*, G. Gaymer Martin
___HP597 *Let My Heart Go*, B. Huston
___HP598 *More Than Friends*, T. H. Murray
___HP601 *Timing is Everything*, T. V. Bateman
___HP602 *Dandelion Bride*, J. Livingston
___HP605 *Picture Imperfect*, N. J. Farrier
___HP606 *Mary's Choice*, Kay Cornelius
___HP609 *Through the Fire*, C. Lynxwiler
___HP610 *Going Home*, W. E. Brunstetter
___HP613 *Chorus of One*, J. Thompson
___HP614 *Forever in My Heart*, L. Ford
___HP617 *Run Fast, My Love*, P. Griffin
___HP618 *One Last Christmas*, J. Livingston
___HP621 *Forever Friends*, T. H. Murray
___HP622 *Time Will Tell*, L. Bliss
___HP625 *Love's Image*, D. Mayne
___HP626 *Down From the Cross*, J. Livingston
___HP629 *Look to the Heart*, T. Fowler
___HP630 *The Flat Marriage Fix*, K. Hayse
___HP633 *Longing for Home*, C. Lynxwiler
___HP634 *The Child Is Mine*, M. Colvin
___HP637 *Mother's Day*, J. Livingston
___HP638 *Real Treasure*, T. Davis
___HP641 *The Pastor's Assignment*, K. O'Brien
___HP642 *What's Cooking*, G. Sattler

(If ordering from this page, please remember to include it with the order form.)

Presents

Great Inspirational Romance at a Great Price!

Heartsong Presents books are inspirational romances in
contemporary and historical settings, designed to give you an
enjoyable, spirit-lifting reading experience. You can choose
wonderfully written titles from some of today's best authors like
Andrea Boeshaar, Wanda E. Brunstetter, Yvonne Lehman, Joyce
Livingston, and many others.

When ordering quantities less than twelve, above titles are $2.97 each.
Not all titles may be available at time of order.

SEND TO: **Heartsong Presents** Readers' Service
          P.O. Box 721, Uhrichsville, Ohio 44683

Please send me the items checked above. I am enclosing $ _____
(please add $3.00 to cover postage per order. OH add 7% tax. NJ
add 6%). Send check or money order, no cash or C.O.D.s, please.
          To place a credit card order, call 1-740-922-7280.

NAME _____

ADDRESS _____

CITY/STATE _____ ZIP_____

HP 9-07